MINE

(A Dark Erotic Romance Novel)

By

Aubrey Dark

For my husband

Names mean nothing, and mine most of all. Call me Rien.

People come to me for plastic surgery, and I cut the fakeness right out of them. It's not my fault that sometimes, when I'm done, there's nothing left.

I left my family a long time ago. They were bad people. Maybe worse than me, if that's possible. But I don't mind my past. The present is all that matters, and my life is perfect.

Absolutely perfect.

CHAPTER ONE

Rien

The man on the operating table moaned softly and stirred, his eyes still closed. A blue plastic cap covered his hair and a blue plastic sheet covered his body. The only things exposed were his face and his chest, straps holding him steady.

"He's almost awake," Gav said. He was standing on the other side of the operating room table.

"Hand me that hypodermic, would you?"

Gav leaned over and gave me the needle. I inserted it into the man's IV on his wrist. Now that he was strapped down nicely to the table, a gag in his mouth, I could bring him out of the anesthesia cleanly.

It was early morning, and the operating room was dim, the way I liked it. Light jazz floated through the room from the stereo system. Mood music for murder.

As the stimulant ran into the man's veins, his eyes opened. He looked at me, then tried to move his arm. Of course, he couldn't.

"What kind of straps are those?" Gav asked.

"Standard nylon," I said. "I get them from the medical supply wholesaler online."

"Hmm. Not leather?"

"You know, I used to do leather. It's hard to get the blood out, though."

"Right. I forget that you get them here when they're still conscious."

The man's eyes flashed back and forth between me

and Gav, questioning. I could see the fear beginning to come through on his face. He knew that this wasn't normal operating procedure for plastic surgery. He opened his mouth to talk, and I tamped the gag down a bit farther into his mouth.

"Don't worry," I said. "This is just a friend of mine. He's going to be here for the surgery. I hope you don't mind."

The man frowned and yelled something through the gag.

"Sorry, Bob. I can't hear you."

"Is his name Bob?" Gav asked.

"Who cares? He'll be dead in a few minutes."

Bob shrieked behind the fabric. I turned back to Gav.

"The nylon straps. I can hook you up with some if you need. If you decide to get back in the business."

Gav sighed and looked down at the man on the table. Bob was trying very hard to talk now, but the gag in his mouth made it awfully difficult. If I had to guess by the look on his face, I'd say he was pleading.

"I'll keep it in mind," he said. "But really, I'm quitting for good this time."

"Quitting for a girl? Say it ain't so, Gavriel. For a girl?"

"You don't know the girl," he said, smiling. He held out a scalpel, the largest one, for the initial cut.

"Want to do the honors?" I asked.

Gav looked down at Bob, who by this time had realized that he was not going to be getting the kind of customer service that men of his status normally got when getting plastic surgery. His muffled yelling rose even louder from behind the gag. I picked up the stereo remote and turned up the volume on the jazz. A low horn sang a dissonant melody under the steady beat of the drums.

"I probably shouldn't," Gav said. His tongue licked his bottom lip, and I knew he wanted to.

"Come on. Just a little cut. You can't go cold turkey."

"Rien…"

"It's not even like you're killing him. Just a cut."

"Okay. Don't tell Kat."

"Tell Kat what?"

"Exactly."

Gav twirled the scalpel in his hand and then lowered the blade to the skin. Bob's muffled cries turned to a high-pitched scream as Gav ran the scalpel across his hairline. Blood ran down both sides of the man's face. I pushed the gag into his mouth farther, and he choked on the scream.

"God, that's good," Gav said. Beads of sweat glistened on his upper lip. He looked down at the scalpel which was dripping blood and offered it to me. I smiled and shook my head.

"Don't stop. We need a chest incision."

"I can't do it all." He wanted to, I could tell. Oh, he wanted to.

"I have another couple coming in tomorrow afternoon," I said, waving the scalpel away. "Please."

"Are you sure?"

"Of course."

"What's that?"

"This?" I asked, holding up the saw. "Los Angeles Police-grade forensic bone saw. Jake got it for me."

"Is he still in the game?"

"Everyone's still in the game, Gav. Everyone but you."

"Yeah, yeah, I know. Shut up."

Gav moved down to the man's bare chest, ignoring his screams. As he cut into the skin, I used forceps to pull back the skin and clamped down the retractor to hold the incision open. The man's heart was beating quickly. Almost in time with the high hats in the song. Maybe with a few more cuts, we would get there.

I waited as Gav worked his magic, cutting back the tendons and fat. He was a delicate surgeon. Almost as good as me. It was a shame he'd given up working. On one level, though, I understood it. After so many victims, sometimes you needed a break to rekindle the passion for the work, so to speak. I doubted he would retire completely, though. He was too good a murderer to give it up.

"Here, take it," Gav said, setting the scalpel down onto the plastic sheet. "I can't finish him."

"Aw, really?"

"Really," he sighed.

"This girl really has her claws in you," I said, picking up the scalpel and twirling it between my fingers. "Making you quit cold turkey like that."

"She's an angel," Gav said. Sincerity bloomed on his face. He was such an innocent serial killer. I could read his face like a medical textbook.

"An angel? Really?"

"I love her. I trust her."

I laughed.

"You can't trust anyone. Even a woman. *Especially* a woman."

"She saved my life."

"Oh? So I have her to blame for your continued friendship." I grinned. "When do I get to meet her?"

Gav looked at me uncertainly.

"Don't you go after her, now," he said.

"What, to flirt with, or to kill?"

"Either."

"Oh, come on!"

"Rien…"

"I won't! I won't. You know I only want you to be

happy."

"Mmhmm."

"And sometimes cutting a man's heart out is what makes you happy. What's wrong with that?"

A squeal came from behind the gag.

"That's what I've been trying to decide. Whether or not I need to keep on…doing what I do," Gav said.

"I say do whatever makes you happy. Do what you love, and you'll never work a day in your life, you know? But if you ever need a break from being a good little boy, you're welcome to come visit me here."

"Thanks, Rien. That's really thoughtful of you."

I smiled.

"Anytime."

CHAPTER TWO

Sara

God, I didn't want to work today.

The bar I worked at to make ends meet was a shitty dive on the corner of La Brea and Sunset. It used to be a spot for rising actors to hang out, and the wood walls were covered in autographed prints of movie stars and rock musicians. Nowadays, though, there weren't any rising actors, only people who pretended they were actors while working shitty jobs on the side. It was the cheapest place to get shots in West Hollywood, and so only the cheapest people came there.

I hated having to listen to their swaggering bullshit about how their next gig was going to be the big one. I hated acting like I cared, despite it being the only acting job I'd had in a while. Most of all, though, I hated cleaning up the puke off of the bathroom floor after all the fake Ernest Hemingways had tossed up their whiskey sours.

"Hey Mark," I said, swinging around to the back of the bar. I surveyed the floor. There were a half-dozen people sipping on drinks at the bar, and only two tables were full.

"Sara, why are you here? Didn't you get Marcy's text?"

"What? What text?" I dug out my phone from my pocket. "No text."

"Marcy, you were fucking supposed to text Sara!" Mark yelled back into the kitchen at his wife.

"I'm busy prepping!" Marcy yelled back.

"Prepping what? We have two tables full."

"Fuck you, Mark!" Marcy yelled. "How about you do your own fucking job and let me do mine?"

"Whatever," I said, not wanting to get them into another endless argument. "What was she supposed to text me?"

"We don't need you tonight," Mark said.

"What?" My heart sank. Had God heard me say I didn't want to work? I didn't mean it. I swear, God, I didn't mean it. I had been counting on at least fifty bucks' worth of tips to make rent at the end of the week.

Mark shook his rag at the customers.

"There just isn't enough money coming in to make it worth it. You understand."

"Who's gonna run the bar?" I asked, waving my hand in the air. I wasn't completely worried, but I was close to it.

"Me," Mark said. "I'm running bar."

"You're the door," I said.

"And?"

"You need someone behind the bar. Or else how can you do door?"

"Nobody's coming through the door, that's the fucking problem," Mark said. "Anyway, the only underage beaners we get coming in, I can toss them out just as quick."

"Jesus, Mark." I didn't know whether to be more upset that he was taking my job, or that he wasn't bothering to hide his racism from me anymore.

"Here's your schedule for next week," he said, pushing the paper across the bartop to me. I scanned the page.

"Nothing until Friday?" Panic burst up inside of me. Oh, dear God. You have such a sense of humor. I was really not going to make rent if I couldn't work all week.

"Are you shitting me?"

"Only crowd we get is weekends."

"Not even Sunday? How about doing a Tuesday ladies' night?" I said, casting about in my mind for a way to fix this. "That usually gets a crowd."

"That usually loses us money," Mark said. "Nobody comes back on other nights. We can't afford to run them anymore."

"Fuck," I said. *"Fuck."*

"I know," Mark said sympathetically. He glanced back at the kitchen door, then shuffled around behind the bar. He brought out a half-empty pint of Jack Daniels.

"Here," he said, pushing the bottle at me. "I'll see you on Friday."

"What, you can't give me work but you can get me drunk?"

"Hey, if you don't want it…"

"I'll take it," I said, grabbing the bottle off of the bartop. "I'm gonna have to find another job for weekdays, I guess."

"I'll give you a good reference if you need it," Mark said. "You've been a good worker. All those damn illegal immigrants taking our jobs."

"Sure, whatever," I said, rolling my eyes as I turned away. "See you Friday."

I walked down the street in a daze. I had no idea what I could do to scrounge up the cash for rent. The late fee was some bullshit like a hundred dollars, and I really couldn't afford to pay that on top of my already shitty rent.

"Well, fuck everything," I said, unscrewing the top of the bottle of Jack. If I didn't have a job anymore, at least I could get drunk.

Sometimes I envied all of the Los Angeles crazies out on the street. They could do whatever they wanted to without pretending to be something they weren't. I took another swig of Jack and watched as a man dressed in tights and fairy wings walked by, singing to himself.

I'd been on the street before. It wasn't fun, but at least it wasn't fake. I'd made that trade a while ago.

For a brief second, I thought about calling my mom and asking for some of the extra cash I'd already sent her way this month. But no. I couldn't ask for it back. Last I'd heard, she was barely keeping afloat with trying to send my sister to community college.

My little sis, getting her degree. That was good. Maybe somebody in my stupid family would make something out of themselves. It certainly wasn't me – failed actress, failed bartender. My mom always told me how proud she was. I wished that I could do something that she would actually be proud of. But the bar was set pretty low on that end.

My phone rang. It was Blaise. Shit. I grimaced as I put the phone to my ear.

"Hey sweetheart, what are you doing tonight?"

"Tonight?"

"Yeah. I got these reservations for Bertesci's. Great place, my dad knows the owner. What do you say? Seven o'clock?"

I'd promised myself that I wouldn't go out on another date with him. He was a grade-A asshole, Hollywood's finest. So full of himself that his ego was spilling out of his ears.

But hey, it was dinner, and I needed my grocery money for rent. I summoned up the ghosts of Stanislavski and Meisner. I'd need all of my acting chops to keep from smacking him across the face before the appetizers came.

"I'd love to!"

"Great," he said. "Wear something tight. Not like that last dress you wore to our date, though. This place is classy."

I wasn't sure dinner was worth this. I gritted my teeth and put on my brightest, happiest voice.

"Sure, Blaise, can't wait!"

Rien

I looked down into Bob's chest. His heart was racing; it had overtaken the beat of the song already. I looked into his face and smiled.

"I'm sorry we can't get to know each other better, Bob," I said. "We haven't even had a proper conversation yet. I would normally have a much better bedside manner, Bob. But I have another client coming in, so we really need to get this finished up quickly."

The man's eyes widened and his screams turned into one high-pitched whine behind the gag. His body twisted against the nylon straps, but they held tight. Good straps. They weren't even that expensive.

I looked down at the heart. A tangle of thick veins and arteries surrounded the beating muscle.

"Which one should I cut?" I asked Gav, winking.

"Make it a show," he said. "I haven't seen blood in a while."

"Sure," I said, bending down and finding the main arterial vessel. I slipped the blade underneath and flicked it up, sending a spray of thick blood into the air above the operating room table. The man's screams faded as his blood spurted in time to the end of the jazz tune, pumping the life out of him. "Like the motherfucking Bellagio fountains."

"Beautiful," Gav said. His face shone with pleasure. "Thanks for letting me sit in."

"Anytime, quitter," I said. "What else are friends for?"

CHAPTER THREE

"Hollywood is so fake, don't you think?" Blaise leaned across the table and refilled my wine glass with whatever expensive Pinot Noir blend he'd bought to impress me this time. I was beginning to think that he just liked to flirt with sommeliers.

"Mmm," I murmured in assent. I couldn't tell a Versailles Merlot from two-buck Chuck, honestly. It all tasted the same to me.

Which was fine, because I couldn't afford to drink anything on my own dime, two-buck Chuck or otherwise. So I smiled and nodded and let guys take me out to fancy places if they wanted to. And Blaise wanted to. I don't think he would ever eat at a place where you *couldn't* get valet parking.

"All of these fake models and fake actresses thinking that they're hot shit, strutting around like they're hot shit. They're not, not really," he said, waving the wine bottle in the air for emphasis. "That's why I like you, Sara."

Really?

"Because I'm not hot shit?"

"Because you don't pretend to be hot shit," he said. "You don't pretend to be this skinny beautiful perfect being."

"That's... pretty rude, Blaise. Insulting, really." What was it about guys nowadays? They felt like they had to put a girl down so that she would drool over them. I hated it.

"You know what I mean," he said. "I saw this girl on Santa Monica today in the tightest dress: bleached blond hair, legs like toothpicks, tits out to here!" He held his hands in front of him. "Who does she think she's impressing?"

"She made an impression on you, didn't she?"

"You know what I mean. What I'm saying is, there are too many fake people in this town."

"Mmmhmm. Are you fake, too?"

"Me?" Blaise looked offended. "I hope not. What do you think?"

I shrugged.

"I don't think I know you well enough to tell if you're fake."

"Sara! I'm hurt."

"Why? It's only our third date."

"You can't tell the difference between me and a total phony? I would think you'd be able to know that right off the bat. I know I can spot a phony in this town right away. My dad works with so many phonies. All of them trying to get something from you. All total fakes."

"I don't know," I said, swirling the wine around in my glass. After losing the one job that paid regularly, I was starting to wonder if I should have come to L.A. in the first place. Every guy I'd met here reminded me of Blaise. "Can you ever really know someone?"

"Is that the aspiring actress in you talking? *Aren't we all just wearing masks?*"

"Well yeah, kinda," I said. "I mean, aren't you?"

"Is that serious? Are you asking that question seriously?"

"Sure. Why not?"

"*Why not?*" Blaise sputtered. "I am *not* fake."

I thought it was stupid for him to deny something so obvious. Most people in Hollywood were fake. Hell, I hadn't done anything real in years. No real relationships. No real friendships. Even the potted plant on my balcony was fake. I didn't hide it. Hollywood wasn't about reality.

"You never pretend?" I asked. "Not even when you pretend to like someone? Or when you act like you're not hurt?"

"No! That's the same thing as lying!"

"So when that seagull shit in my hair on our second date and you said it didn't bother you after I wiped it off, even though you kept staring at that spot on my head the whole time and it *obviously* bothered you…"

"That was different. Being nice is different than faking."

"Not if you're faking being nice."

"You know what I mean!" he cried in exasperation.

Okay, so Blaise was an idiot. For the first couple of dates, I'd thought that maybe his offhand insults and idiotic remarks were just him being nervous. This was our… third? date, though, and he hadn't gotten any better. Shame, too. The guy was cute. Arrogant and stupid, but cute.

His phone buzzed and he reached over to check it.

"Sorry, it's a work thing," he said, tapping away on his phone. I didn't know if this was also a ruse to impress me, or if he really was such a workaholic he had to check his email every time a new one hit his inbox. What did he do, anyway? Some kind of sales job at one of the major studios, I vaguely remembered. His dad had gotten him the job. And the car to go with it.

Most people in Hollywood slept around with people who worked at studios. They used sex to get a better audition, a better part, a better paycheck. The main problem with sleeping around in Hollywood is that people think you're sleeping around for the wrong reasons, not just to, you know, sleep around. But I liked sex. Sometimes I'd be talking about my latest date, and the friend listening to me would nod their head knowingly. They all thought I went to bed with men to get ahead.

Truth of it was, I'd never had sex with anyone I didn't want to have sex with. I wouldn't let myself do that, not ever.

But none of the guys I slept with impressed me. Not that they were all porn stars doing crazy kinky shit. If anything, the guys in Hollywood were too vanilla for me. I wanted the real kind of good sex, the kind where you explore all the ways to make each other feel good. The guys in L.A. were weirdly hung up about sex, though. They only wanted to fuck in positions that made them look good. They didn't want to get messy. They needed their hair to stay styled and perfect. That was more important to them than good sex.

Take Blaise here. He could be a sex god. That's why I had let him pick me up at the club, anyway. He had the looks and the physique, and a face that wasn't movie-star handsome, but better than most. And really big hands. I'd hoped that meant what it usually meant.

I imagined those bulging muscles, naked and oiled, his chest broad and heavy, writhing in silk sheets as we twisted around each other. His thick hands gripping me around the wrists and pinning me down as he fucked me so hard the plaster rained down from the ceiling.

Three dates in, and he hadn't made a move other than kissing me goodnight last time. I'd tried to get more from him. I'd let my hand brush against the front of his pants, hoping that there would be a thick erection there just waiting to burst out of his underwear. But nope. Nothing. Nada. One kiss and a goodnight.

Such a letdown. I know I wasn't as perfect looking as most of the girls in L.A.—the technical term for a plain Jane like me is "character actor"—but I had a lot to offer guys, or so I thought. But I guessed for Blaise I was just the backup girl he could take out to one of his dad's clubs whenever he needed somebody on his arm.

I picked up my phone and checked my email as I sipped the Pinot Noir and waited for Blaise to stop impressing me with his dedication to work. One new email. I checked the sender.

The casting director for MGM! It must be a message about my last audition. I had done super well. My agent had landed me this sweet audition for a supporting role in a new TV police drama. The role was for a sassy undercover agent out on the streets of Chicago. I'd nailed it. It was *such* a good part, too!

My heart began to beat faster as I opened the email.

Dear Sara Everett, we are sorry to inform you...

Fuck.

Double fuck.

I slumped back in my seat as my eyes skimmed the rest of the form rejection. A sigh escaped my lips.

"What's the matter?" Blaise asked, putting his phone down and shoving a forkful of strawberry goat cheese salad into his mouth. "Gomf some bad newsh?"

"Close your mouth when you chew, why don't you," I said, irritated all over. He raised his eyebrows and swallowed the goat cheese.

"Don't scowl," he said. "It makes your forehead wrinkle. Got some bad news?"

"Yes, as a matter of fact," I said, setting down my wine. "I didn't get this part for a TV show. I really wanted it. The script needed some work, but damn, I really wanted it."

"Everybody really wants. You know what I mean?"

"No shit, but I thought I did *really* well. I can't believe I didn't get it."

"Yeah, yeah. Everybody thinks—"

"Fuck you," I said, cutting him off. I didn't want to listen to any of his bullshit right now.

"What?" Blaise let his fork clatter to his plate. "I was just trying to make you feel better."

"You know what?" I said. "The next time you're gonna say something to make me feel better, stick a cock in your mouth instead."

His mouth dropped open.

"Just like that," I said. "Only with a big fat cock right… there."

He closed his mouth with an audible snap. I shoveled salad into my mouth and took another bread roll from the center of the table. If this date was going off the tracks, I needed to eat quickly. I didn't have any food in my shithole apartment for a dinner tonight.

"Maybe if you got a decent agent, you'd get some parts," Blaise said, a frown creasing his face. He didn't look nearly as handsome when he frowned.

"I have an agent."

"You have a washed-up old man who calls you when the casting directors can't get anyone off the D-list to come to their auditions."

"Fuck you," I said. "Roger is great." I wished I hadn't told Blaise about my agent. Or the audition. Or anything. This date was a disaster from the beginning.

"Roger is a has-been. Everybody in Hollywood knows that."

"He's a great agent."

He wasn't a great agent. I knew that. But Roger had taken me in when I first arrived in California, and he'd given me advice and a place to stay while I got on my feet. I owed him. After this audition, though, I was beginning to think that maybe I should switch to another agent. I just didn't know how to tell Roger. It would break his heart.

"Maybe you should go fuck him, then," Blaise said.

"Maybe I will, since your dick doesn't ever seem to be working."

"Are you fucking kidding me?" The veins on his temples were throbbing.

"Are you?"

"So it's my fault? Just because I don't assume I'm getting laid? Just because I try to treat you like a lady? Or did you want me to fuck you on our first date like a classless whore?"

That word. I gripped the table, trying not to slap him.

"I can make my own decisions about whether or not to fuck you on the first date. Or the second. Or the third. Right now, I'm not sure you even have the proper equipment down there."

"Fine! See if I ever try to take you to dinner again!" Blaise said, throwing his napkin on the table. The wine sommelier had come over with the next bottle of wine Blaise had ordered for us. Hearing our conversation, he started to turn away. I grabbed his coattails and he turned right back.

"It's okay," I said. "I was about to leave, but I'm sure Blaise would love to have the bottle to himself. Maybe you two could chat about the vintages, just the two of you."

"Fuck you," Blaise hissed. "You're a shitty wanna-be actress with a wanna-be agent who can't wait to whore herself out."

"Keep buying expensive wines," I said. "Maybe all the antioxidants will make your dick grow longer. Or maybe you'll just drink your tears away."

"Ah... ahem," the sommelier said.

"Bye. I hope the two of you have a long and happy life together," I said.

"You're just as fake as the rest of Hollywood," Blaise sputtered. His face was beet-red, and his hands clutched the tablecloth. I leaned over and plucked a dinner roll from the bread basket and tucked it into my purse. Breakfast for tomorrow.

"We're all fake," I said. "Me, I'm the only one who doesn't pretend to be real."

CHAPTER FOUR

Sara

I was most of the way through the bottle of Jack Daniels when my phone rang. I squinted hard at the screen. It was my agent, Roger.

I didn't really want to talk to him right then, but maybe it was for the best. That audition had been the last thing I had going for me in the past month. If he couldn't find me any parts, maybe it was time to move onto another agent. As dumb as he was, maybe Blaise was right about that. I took a deep breath and answered the phone.

"Hey, Roger, what's up?" I asked.

"Sara, my darling!" he said, with an overenthused joyfulness that I could tell was fake. His voice was whiskey-grizzled, and I wondered if he was drunk right now. "How did that audition go?"

"I didn't get it," I said. "I mean, the audition went well. I guess it just wasn't my part. The dialogue was clunky, anyway. Listen, Roger—"

"Never mind that," he said. "I have another part for you. Guaranteed."

"Guaranteed?" I tried not to let the skepticism show in my voice. And I tried not to let the tiny flicker of hope in my heart grow. If there was one thing in this city that was poison, it was hopes and dreams.

"The studio contacted me directly," he said. "Asked if I had a girl meeting a certain criteria. And you would fit the part perfectly!"

"What was the criteria?"

"They wanted the best Method actor I had," he said. "You have to sink into this role completely. It's an improv-type thing, they said, and you have to be willing to commit to the part for a full day. I thought to myself: who does Method acting like a champ? Sara! It has to be her!"

"Only a day?" I asked suspiciously.

"Tomorrow. That's why they contacted me. Wanted someone who would be able to jump right into the role."

You mean they wanted someone desperate, I thought. They must be filling in for someone who dropped out. Well, I was desperate.

"I can do tomorrow," I said. "What time?"

"Eight in the morning. You'll meet the client at the Starbucks right near Paramount. You know the one on Van Ness Avenue?"

"Is it a Paramount movie part?"

"They didn't say, but that's the guy who called me. He works there."

The little flicker of hope inside me began to flame up. I took a swig of Jack to dampen it back down.

"What kind of a part is it? Do you have any other information? What should I wear?"

"Sorry, they didn't give me much about it. Sounds like a one-shot thing. Nothing long term."

"Ah. Boo."

"If you're not interested—"

"No, I am! I am," I said. "I was just hoping to go there prepared."

"They said they'd prepare you on-set," Roger said, sounding so confident that I actually began to think that this was a job I would get if I just showed up. Hell, even if it was a walk-on role as an extra, they'd pay me fifty dollars and I'd get to scavenge the snack table for lunch. A warmth spread through my chest that could have been a newfound sense of hopefulness. It could also have been the Jack Daniels. I didn't mind either way.

"Thank you so much, Roger!" I said. "I'll let you know how it goes."

"Sure, sure," he said, his attention already waning. "I'll be out next week for an agent conference, but I'm sure you'll do just fine."

"Thanks again," I said. "You're the best."

"Of course I am, kid. Hey. Break a leg."

Rien

It was the next morning before I dealt with the cleanup. I always sleep better when there's a body in the house. Even if it's dead.

I checked my watch. It was only ten. If I worked quickly, I could crack this guy's skull open and still have time to watch an episode of *Sherlock* while I ate lunch. Excellent. Humming along to the bass line, I picked up my mallet and tossed it up in a spin, catching it again on the downbeat. *Ready to go.*

Jazz is good for killing, but the cleanup afterwards always puts me in more of a post-rock sort of mood. Something with a weird beat, something to keep my head bobbing.

Most serial killers save trophies from their victims. Gav never did, the damn quitter, but most of us do. Some of us take the victim's jewelry. Some of us keep locks of hair, or fingernails, or fingers. I heard of one guy who clipped the Garfield comic from that day's copy of the New York Times every time he killed.

Me, I'm working on a sculpture.

It's in the front of my waiting room inside of a glass

globe. I'm sure my patients have no idea what it is, and none of them have ever commented on it. I suppose when you're getting ready to have your face cut open, there's no time to waste looking at art.

If they looked closer, though, they would see that the plastic sculpture is made out of smaller parts, almost like a fractal. Each part is a thin sheet of tissue.

Specifically, human tissue.

Even more specifically, the tissue that makes up the part of the brain known as the claustrum, the little bit of gray matter in our skulls that turns our consciousness on and off.

That's right. I'm making brain art.

The man's skull was already exposed at the hairline where Gav had made his first cut. I peeled that layer back and pinned it down. I could see the ridge where I wanted to put the chisel. I set the pointed edge into the crack between the skull plates and whacked it with the mallet. The *pop!* sound of the skull cracking into two was so satisfying. Like cracking open a walnut.

I had to move fast. This part was what kids call *gross*, even for a surgeon. Brain matter is hard to work with. It falls apart in your hands like the cheap knockoff Jello they serve in hospitals. But the skull plates pulled back easily, and now I was close. The feds might want the teeth back, for proof. But I didn't want teeth.

I wanted my trophy.

CHAPTER FIVE

Sara

The coffeeshops near Paramount are filled with hack writers churning out their next screenplay. Everybody thinks they're going to be the next big thing, and everybody is wrong. Eighty percent of movies nowadays are sequels or adaptations. Nothing's new under the sun. Original and daring doesn't sell. It's depressing, but I try not to think about it too much. I always figured that if I got a part in *Fast and Furious 23: Faster Than Peregrine Falcons*, I'd be able to convince the writers to do some real dialogue. Not that terrible one-liner shit that passes for writing nowadays.

As I walked through the tables filled with Apple laptops and jackets with elbow patches sewn on for looks, I tugged on the hem of my dress, looking around for the man I was supposed to meet. I hoped he would buy me a coffee; I couldn't afford overpriced lattes.

I spotted him in the back of the coffeeshop instantly. He was the only one dressed in a business suit, and he had a black leather bag sitting on the table in front of him. Definitely not a writer. I plastered on a smile and headed back.

"Hi, I'm Sara," I said. I slid into the chair opposite him. He looked nervous, almost angry.

"Stand back up," he ordered.

"Um, sure," I said. Awkwardly, I stood up again, hands at my sides. He looked me up and down, squinting at me like I was a cantaloupe he had been sent to pick up from the grocery store.

"Did you want me to read some lines?" I asked, after a couple of seconds.

"What color are your eyes?"

"Green," I said. As if he couldn't see for himself.

"Brown hair, green eyes. I asked for blue eyes. You don't have blue eyes."

"Sorry," I said. "If it's that important for the part, I can get contact lenses."

"Yes," he said, seemingly distracted. He didn't stop looking at me, evaluating every part. "Yes, we'll have to do that. I asked for big, but… you're bigger than her. Wider. In the hips."

Roger hadn't told me they asked for a fat chick. I guess it made sense, though.

"Thanks," I said, pressing my lips together so that I didn't blurt out something sarcastic that would cost me the part. I was used to casting directors commenting on my body, even for roles that asked for curvy girls. "I can act, too."

"Huh? Oh. Yes. Right. Yes, you'll need to do that."

He looked me up and down one more time, then nodded.

"You'll do."

"Thanks," I said again, grinding my teeth. "Roger said this was a one-day part."

"Yes," the man said. "We'll start now."

He stood up and began walking to the door. I followed him. So much for him buying me coffee.

"There's a dress shop down the street here," he said. "We'll see if some clothes will make the difference."

"Okay. What kind of a part is this?"

"Later," the man said. "I'll explain later."

"Okay, but I'd like to know, you know, how much the pay is, what I'm going to be doing. Union rules—"

"Yes, yes," the man said. He darted a quick look

down one side of the street, and then took my arm and began walking the other way. "Later. My guy said you were a method actor."

"That's right," I said, feeling inordinately proud. I wasn't just the chubby brown-haired girl. I was the chubby brown-haired girl that took her acting very seriously.

We walked quickly down the street toward the dress shop, stopping in a drugstore to pick up some cheap colored contacts. I wish I could say that mornings in L.A. were refreshing, but the smell of piss really comes out of the alleyways once the sun rises. The man couldn't stop looking back over his shoulder.

"Do you have a stalker?" I asked.

"Excuse me?" The man's face froze in something like fear.

"Do you have a stalker? The way you're looking behind us at every corner, I thought maybe your ex-wife might be joining us with a knife."

I swear to God, this guy's face went dead white. He looked like he'd just seen a ghost. What kind of a job was this? I was beginning to reconsider staying with Roger as an agent.

"Let's go inside," he said, coughing through his words and avoiding my curious gaze.

"This place?" I asked, looking up at the storefront. It was one of the most expensive couture shops in West Hollywood. Not the discount costume racks I was used to when I played an extra. My curiosity level bumped up one notch.

"This place."

I must have tried on every dress in the shop, and some more they had hidden behind the counter. The saleswoman gushed over each one, but the man stood in front of the dressing room critically, arms crossed, and rejected them one after another.

"Too sexy."

"Too bold."

"That's not her style."

I wanted to ask who *she* was, what kind of character I would be playing. The thought crossed my mind that maybe this guy wanted to take me somewhere as his escort. That would explain why he was dressing me up in such fancy clothes.

"That one. That one's perfect."

I looked up at the dressing room mirror. I had to agree with him. The dress was a dark navy A-line cut with a boatneck collar. It came down to just above my knee and hugged my curves loosely at the hips, accentuating my hourglass figure. The navy pumps had a bit of a wedge, giving me some more height than normal. I turned sideways and preened. *This* was the kind of thing I should be wearing to auditions. Classy, but not ostentatious. Sexy, but not like a hooker. It was perfect.

"This belt would go perfectly," the saleswoman said, hooking the gold-braided patterned belt around my waist. It clinked softly as it settled against the fabric.

"We'll take it," the man said decisively.

"Do you have earrings that would match?" I asked. The saleswoman scuttled off to find them.

"Earrings?" the man asked, frowning. "I don't know if she wears earrings."

"Trust me, she wears earrings," I said. I didn't know what this character was, but if she wore this dress, she would definitely wear earrings.

"Fine," the man grumbled. "Leave the dress on, and cut the tags off." He took out his credit card and left it on the counter. I turned sideways in the dress, admiring myself and fixing my hair. He went to make a phone call while the saleswoman rang up the purchase.

"All set?"

He held out his arm, and I tucked my hand into the crook of his elbow. So what if I was playing an escort? I could get into that role. I could get into any role.

Outside of the dress shop, a black sedan idled.

"This is our ride," the man said, opening the back door. "Get in."

I hesitated for a moment. Wasn't this how horror movies started? A woman getting into an unmarked black sedan with some rich guy she didn't know? This guy hadn't even told me his name yet. What if he wasn't from Paramount? What if he was taking me out to the back woods to kill me and wear my skin? Okay, okay, so I had an overactive imagination, but still.

"I'll explain everything," the man said, his finger tapping against his thigh. "Once we're on our way."

"Look, I just want to know what I'm getting paid," I said. A fifty dollar extra role wasn't worth this risk, and even though I was curious who this guy was, I had to go out and find another job.

"One thousand dollars," the man said. "In cash."

"Okay, then," I said, sliding into the back of the car before he could change his mind. I didn't know what I was doing, but Roger had just gotten me the best paid gig I'd had in years. And if the guy turned out to be a murderer, well, maybe I could escape and sell the story rights to Paramount. Win-win.

CHAPTER SIX

Rien

I cut through the brain, paring away the outside layers. The claustrum is down on the very underside of the neocortex. Right in the center of the brain. It's amazing how our bodies try to protect us from being turned off, it really is.

I used the small scalpel to carve out that little curved piece of brain tissue. Gently, gently, I put the center of Bob's consciousness on the metal surgical plate. It was a perfect specimen, the tissue as thin and unblemished as any I've ever come across. I smiled.

Bob was a typical Los Angeles businessman, I imagined. Faker than a three-dollar bill. His suit was a cheap Armani knock-off. I didn't even mind sending it down into the incinerator with him. But he must have messed with the wrong people.

You only get sent to me if you mess with the wrong people.

The small chunk of brain went into the formaldehyde bath. I took Bob's body and shoved it down into the incinerator, the surgical drapes going right in after him. You might think the smell of burning human flesh is bad, but really the plastic sheeting smells much worse. I lit a vanilla-scented candle and went back to work on my trophy.

The brain tissue was set, and I took it out of the formaldehyde with gloved hands. The next step was tricky. I put the tissue in a acetone bath and stuck it in the freezer. The acetone would suck out the organic tissue and replace it with acetone. This would take a while, but I had other things to do.

Like cleaning up the blood.

The song playing on the stereo transitioned to a faster beat, and I moved to the rhythm of the music as I got the brand-new mop out of the closet. Bleach and water and a nice mopping. The smell of the bleach mixed with the vanilla bean. Sterile, but homey. Just the way I liked it. The mop smeared the blood over the white tile, then soaked it up. Three passes with a new bucket each time, and the tile grout was pristine.

Four hours to go.

I took the brain tissue out of the acetone bath. It was frozen, the crinkles in the brain fixed eternally in the position it had been in when Bob had died. This was the last step. I transferred it into another tub, this one filled with epoxy resin. It was the same stuff that you would put on your hardwood floors, if you were as wealthy as my victims. The acetone took the place of the brain, and the epoxy resin would take the place of the acetone. And when it was all done, we'd have a nice plastic copy of the brain. Well, part of the brain. The important part. Francis Crick, the man who helped discover DNA, said that the claustrum was like "a conductor coordinating a group of players in the orchestra." I liked that.

I liked it so much, I had collected seventy-two of them.

Sara

. The man shut the privacy window between us and the driver. He pulled out the drugstore bag and gave it to me. Blue contact lenses.

"Put these in," he said. I did as he asked. My heart raced. One thousand dollars? I blinked, the eye drops running down my cheeks. The windows were tinted. Was this a sex thing? I didn't know if I could handle it if Roger had accidentally set me up with somebody who wanted to hire a prostitute.

"Fix your makeup," the man said, handing me a mirror. "And put all of your belongings in this bag."

"Okay, but could you tell me please what's going on here?" I asked. The car pulled away from the curb and began to drive down Van Ness Avenue.

"I'm sorry for all the secrecy," the man said. "My name is Gary Steadhill."

"I'm Sara Everett," I said, holding my hand out for a handshake. He didn't take it.

"No," he said. "Today you're not Sara."

"I'm not?"

"Today you're Mrs. Susan Steadhill."

I blinked hard. The man was looking at me cautiously, waiting to see what I would say.

"So, is this some kind of sexual role play?" I asked. "Because I was told—"

"No, no, nothing like that," the man said.

"Then what?"

The man leaned back in his seat and exhaled.

"You've heard of my name before?"

"Gary Steadhill? Sorry, no. Are you with Paramount?"

"I'm a businessman."

"Oh. *Oh.*" The name flashed through my mind, this time in large bolded caps. "Steadhill Tech. That's your company?"

"That's right." He smirked proudly. "See, you have heard my name."

"So are you getting into the movie business?"

"No. That's not what this is. Here is the—ah—the

contract," he said, pulling out a sheet of paper. "Before I say anything more, I'd like you to agree to the terms of secrecy. You can't let anybody know about this role."

Gary took out his wallet and began counting out crisp hundred dollar bills. I skimmed the contract and signed my name at the bottom.

"Okay," I said, eyeing the cash. "Now what?"

"Here. This is half of the money up front. You'll get the rest at the end of today."

My eyes nearly bugged out of my head at how casually he flicked five hundred dollars toward me.

"Great," I said, stuffing the money into the bag with all my stuff. "What next?"

"Next, I need you to pretend to be my wife."

"Susan Steadhill. Right. Why, exactly?"

Gary coughed into his hand and looked out of the tinted window.

"It's a long story," he said. "Remember, you're bound to secrecy."

"Cross my heart and hope to die," I said, a finger over my lips.

"My wife and I were... *are* very public personages. We co-own the business. And recently we've been fighting. Naturally, I can't let the details of our relationship leak to the public."

"Naturally."

"I'm supposed to have a bit of plastic surgery today," he said, shifting uneasily in his chair.

"Surgery?"

"It isn't anything big, I'm getting some moles removed and a bit of a facelift. Susan is supposed to be there, you understand, for liability. She's my medical trustee. And since they're putting me under general anesthesia, she has to be there in case anything goes wrong."

"And your wife can't be there because...?"

"We're not—ah—currently speaking to each other," Gary said, his skin flushing a bit red at his shirt collar.

"You're fighting."

"In a manner of speaking."

"What about?" I wanted to know exactly what it took to make Susan mad.

"That's not—ah—necessary for you to know about."

"I want to get the character right, Mr. Steadhill," I said firmly.

"Yes. Yes, of course you do. Well, I took her to the Santa Monica pier for our anniversary. It was where we first met, you see. And she balked at my idea for our – our vacation. She didn't want to do things my way."

"Hmm." Susan's husband was a bit of a control freak. And Susan was a bit stubborn. Okay, I could do that.

"And I couldn't convince her, and she got mad and we fought." He looked away, obviously embarrassed to be talking about it.

"That's fine. Okay. You couldn't make up before this appointment, though?"

"She's so stubborn," Mr. Steadhill said, frustration running along his browline. "I can't reschedule the procedure; it takes forever to get on this guy's list. So I thought that I would hire someone who looks like Susan to come along."

"Can't you get another person to be your medical… whatever?" I asked. "I mean, don't get me wrong, I want the part. It's just that…what if something does go wrong during the surgery?"

"Nothing will go wrong, of course," he said quickly. "It's a very standard procedure. All you'll have to do is sit in the waiting room until the surgery is done, and then we'll leave together. But I don't want anyone knowing that my wife and I are having trouble. Especially a private surgeon… I've heard horror stories about rumors leaking from medical staff."

"It's easier to just pretend that everything's okay between you two."

"Exactly. Not perfect; we don't have a perfect relationship, but..."

"Normal."

"Yes. Normal." He looked relieved that I understood. I kind of understood, but I suppose I didn't have to understand too much to get paid a grand for acting like a Hollywood wife. "Do you think you can do it?"

"Absolutely," I said, trying to sound like a confident actor. "Tell me more about Susan."

Rien

I dumped the used scalpels, forceps, and retractors into a vat of antiseptic fluid to sterilize them. The incinerator roared, the rumble mixing with the sound of the music playing overhead. I fished a pair of forceps out of the vat and used it to take out the claustrum from the resin. My little plastic piece of brain. I put it in the heater to cure. _Bake at 400 degrees for a half-hour, or until crisp and delicious._

The last album on the playlist started, and I knew I only had a couple of hours left before my next clients came in. I looked around to make sure everything was clean. White tile. New surgical drapes and sheets on the operating table. Check, check, check. I showered. I dressed. I burned my old clothes in the incinerator. Then I went to check on Bob's brain.

After I took the brain tissue out of the oven, I flicked it with my fingernail to make sure it was hardened all the way. Done. It looked like a pink-gray scrap of Kleenex now, and it was ready to add to the others.

I ducked through the door into the waiting room, with its white tile and leather chairs. The waiting room was at the back of my house, only accessible through the alleyway. I'm a very private plastic surgeon. The pinnacle of discretion.

I took the latest edition of *Reader's Digest* and *Better Homes and Gardens* from the mail and set them out on the coffee table. Then I took Bob's little plastic brain tissue and put it inside the glass globe. I tilted my head and peered at the mass of brain tissues, all leaning against each other. Like they were talking to each other.

The word claustrum means "hidden away." I think it's fitting that my secret trophies end up smack dab in the middle of my waiting room, masquerading as modern art. I moved Bob's piece a little to the left so that it abuts the glass. So you could see the main crinkle of his brain from the outside. Yes, that looked much better.

All that work, and everyone just thinks they're little blobs of plastic. Such a shame.

I looked at the clock. It was almost time.

Sara

"So what's my motivation?"

"Motivation?"

I only had a few hours to prepare for the role. We spoke in the back of the car privately and I took notes on Susan.

Part of method acting is sinking into the role completely. When you take on a character, you're not simply acting like the character. You *are* the character. I quizzed Gary on every little detail about his wife that I thought I should know, from her favorite foods and TV shows to her childhood pets. Not surprisingly, Gary didn't know everything about his wife. Little wonder they were on the skids. But I would do the best with what I had.

"You know, my motivation. Desires."

"Desires?"

"Gary, I can't *become* Susan unless I know what she wants. What's her driving motivation? What are her goals? *My* goals? Maybe I want to be a good wife?"

Gary snorted. Okay, so that one was out.

"I need something to work with," I said.

"Alright, how's this? Your motivation is to suck all of the money out of the business and spend it on pedicures and antique furniture while your husband works overtime for you. Your goal is to flirt with every pool boy and waiter and pretend like you don't know what I'm talking about when I confront you at night. Your desire is to appear to the world like you've got it all—the loving family, the mansion on the hill, the high-powered career—even though you have a cold, hateful, spite-filled heart that doesn't let anyone else in. You're a shitty wife and an even shittier businesswoman, and you stab anyone in the back if they're not looking."

Whoa. I guess Gary and Susan really were fighting.

"Okay, then," I said, pretending to take notes. "Got it. Unhappy marriage, pretending like everything's good."

"That stupid bitch," Gary seethed, looking out at the pedestrians along Hollywood Boulevard.

"Can I ask you something?" I asked, hoping to change the subject. "About the surgery procedure?"

"What?"

"You said that I would be the medical trustee if anything goes wrong. So what do you want me to do if anything goes wrong?"

"Nothing will go wrong."

"Yeah, but what if? Do you want, you know, life support? Or—"

"Of course I want life support!" Gary said. "Heroic measures, the works. Don't let them pull the plug. Cost isn't an issue. But nothing will go wrong, trust me."

"Okay, sure. Let's move onto something else," I said. "I think I've got it."

"Good," Gary said, looking at his watch. The sun was getting ready to sink into the smog of the L.A. valley. "It's almost time."

He leaned forward and opened the privacy screen.

"Take us to the surgeon," he said. "We're ready."

CHAPTER SEVEN

Rien

Everything was set up. The instruments were all laid out in order on the medical table, exactly the way I liked them. Tempered steel scalpels, from the wide No.18 chisel blade with a long handle to the tiny No.12 with its crescent blade like a hook. Each one made for its job, each one perfect in its own way.

I held up the largest straight blade to the light. It was sharpened down so that the edge would cut through skin like it was cutting through cheese.

Today the couple would come to me, hoping for a fresh start. Here: this operating room, so clean and white, overlooking the hills of Hollywood. A place to get plastic surgery while maintaining their privacy. And they would get it, alright.

When I was done cutting, they would be gone. The only thing that would remain of them was the emptiness that was there at the beginning.

People have such hollow lives. I'm always surprised when they beg to keep them.

The blade flashed orange, reflecting the sky outside. I set it back down onto the table carefully and admired the view outside of the huge window that made up one whole side of my operating room. It overlooked the west Los Angeles valley, and I had paid a fortune for it. Or rather, my clients had paid a fortune for it.

Sunsets in L.A. were beautiful, especially from my mansion. Fiery red and gold clouds spilled across the sky, and the moon was already visible in the evening dusk. It was a curved sliver of white, as thin and sharp as my scalpels. The operating room, white tile from floor to ceiling, reflected the burning colors of the sky.

I stripped the latex gloves off of my hands and shot them like rubber bands into the trash. Although I didn't technically need the operating room to be sterile, I still liked to keep it clean. I suppose it was an old habit that I'd kept around from medical school and my work as an anesthesiologist. Back when I was doing no harm.

The operating table was white and chrome, and I rested one hand on the side of the table. The chrome was cool under my fingertips. Then my hand jerked back, as though afraid to contaminate the clean bed. I used my shirtsleeve to wipe my fingerprints from the chrome. There. Perfect again.

I looked out the window once more. The sky was already darkening. The clouds had turned ash-gray, dirty shadows of their former fire, and the white tile no longer reflected any color at all.

Sara

We pulled up to a private driveway just off of Sunset. I looked over at Gary. He seemed calm.

"Are we not going to the hospital?" I asked, frowning.

"Hospital?" he asked, looking surprised.

"You know, the place where most people get surgery."

Gary laughed at me. My chest clenched, and I tried to work with it. Susan hated Gary, so I hated Gary. But it was a calm, controlled hatred. Yes.

"You think famous people go to Cedars Sinai to get

work done? Hell, no. That would be way too much publicity. We have a private doctor. They say he's the best. I only hope he keeps his mouth shut."

"Ah," I said, sinking into my role as Susan. Of course we would have a private doctor. Of course.

The car pulled around into an alleyway and stopped behind one of the private estates. There was a gate that opened as our sedan pulled into the back driveway, and then closed behind us. I stared up at the back of the huge mansion. A white door was the only entryway I could see, lit up by a spotlight and the rapidly dimming sun. There were no windows on this side of the house.

"That's it," Gary said. "Are you ready to be Mrs. Susan Steadhill?"

"Yes, *dear*," I said, sneering dismissively.

"Perfect," Gary said, looking at me with approval.

We got out of the car and headed toward the house. I kept my gaze ahead of me, not on Gary. I imagined Susan Steadhill, bored as hell by having to chaperone her husband into plastic surgery. Gary held the door for me and I brushed by without thanking him. I could tell he was impressed by my acting, at least so far. Well, I didn't have to do much, did I?

I walked into what looked like a waiting room. Two of the walls were floor-to-ceiling mirrors that made the room seem much bigger than it was. At the front there was a stand with a piece of art on it that looked interesting. But I was Susan Steadhill, and I didn't know if I cared about art all that much.

Instead, I went straight to one of the leather chairs in the middle of the room and sat down, picking up a magazine. I flipped through the pages of huge houses and manicured lawns. I stopped on an ad for Italian marble countertops. Susan would like this. No, *I* would like this. Maybe I would redecorate my kitchen, I thought. Which marble would I like best? Not the black, that's too modern. A nice antique look. Cream marble with blue French tile for the backsplash. Yes, that would be nice.

Gary had just stepped up to the counter when a door opened from the back and a man dressed in surgical scrubs came out. I peeked over and saw a glimpse of what looked like a hospital room behind him, white tile and IV stands set up next to a metal table. I feigned a yawn and went back to my marble.

"Mrs. Steadhill?"

My eyes snapped up from the magazine. Both men were looking at me.

"Yes?"

"Hi. I'm Dr. Damore, the anesthesiologist for your husband today. I need you to sign these forms, and we'll be ready to go."

Tossing the magazine aside on the table, I got up and went to the counter. It was then that I noticed the doctor. He seemed average when he came through the door, nondescript even, but now that I saw him up close, something about him drew my attention. His eyes weren't brown, as I originally thought, but a golden, tawny color that seemed to change with the tilt of his head. It was a strange look, handsome but not conventional. *A lion*, I thought, the image coming to mind as I looked at him. *A predator*.

I couldn't help but be attracted to him. Or rather, *Susan* was attracted to him. Why wouldn't she be? He was an attractive man. For a brief, stupid instant, I wished that I could meet him again, outside. Somewhere real, where I could introduce myself. There was something about him that drew me forward even as I held myself back.

"Right here, please. And initial down the back."

I picked up the clipboard with the form on it and quickly dashed off a signature. Gary looked nervously at me, and I could tell that he was worried I would trip up on the signature. He had no reason to worry, stupid man. I *was* Susan.

"How long will this take?" I asked, jotting the initials *S.S.* down on each line of the page. I was thinking about later that day, when I would go get a pedicure and spend a few hours visiting with my other trophy wife friends at the wine bar. Maybe I'd stop by the office and meet with an important shareholder. Ho, hum.

"Not long," the doctor said. "An hour or two at the most."

I looked back at him, and in that instant my tongue felt thick in my mouth. He was staring at me as though he could see through the surface, down deep inside of me. I swallowed and shifted my gaze to his hairline, where a sliver of dark brown hair could be seen under his surgical cap..

"Good," I said, trying to regain my original confidence. I handed him the clipboard, and his fingers touched my hand as it passed between us. It was only for a split second, but I felt it like an electrical shock. The pads of his fingers were smooth and delicate, and they stroked the side of my hand. I jerked my hand back, then flipped my hair over my shoulder to pretend like I hadn't felt a thing. Susan hadn't felt a thing.

When I looked up at him, though, he was still staring at me with that gaze that seemed to look right through my mask.

I can see you, it seemed to say. *I can see the real you.*

Rien

"Would you like to come and see the operating room, Mrs. Steadhill?" I asked.

The young woman inclined her head slightly. Her eyes landed on her husband's face, and he shrugged. A small shrug, almost imperceptible.

"Sure," she said, turning back to me. "Why not?"

"Why not, indeed?" I said, motioning them both toward the door. Mr. Steadhill held the door open for her and she passed through briskly. There was something strange about her, I thought. She was different from most of the wives who had come through my doors.

Everybody who came into my operating room was guilty of something. I knew that better than anyone, except maybe Vale or the people who paid my salary. But the way she moved gave me some pause. She wasn't as smooth as I imagined a CEO co-conspirator would be. There was something not quite right about her. Maybe it was the way she looked to her husband for the answer to my question, the way a natural submissive would. She didn't seem like the mastermind type.

Orders were orders, though.

I led them to the operating room table.

"This is the heart monitor, breathing monitor, blood pressure. We'll check all vital stats throughout the procedure to make sure nothing goes wrong. I'll be your anesthesiologist and get you all set up before the surgeon comes in."

I used to be a great anesthesiologist. It had gotten harder and harder as I went. I put people under, and it was getting too tempting to let them stay there if they deserved it. But that was a long time ago.

"Where are the other staff?" Mrs. Steadhill asked. She looked at me with an expression that made me think she knew who I was. There was no way she knew who I was. There was no way she would have walked into my office if she had known.

"No other staff," I said brightly. "It's only me and the surgeon. That's what you're paying for, isn't it? Privacy?"

"Yes," Mr. Steadhill said, walking to the window. "And I hear you're the best at that."

"Absolutely, sir," I said. Out of the corner of my eye, I could see the woman glance at me. Was she suspicious? Or was I paranoid? Maybe she was interested in me. Women often were. Especially married women.

"Nice view you have here," Mr. Steadhill said.

"One-way glass, of course," I said. "We can see them, they can't see us."

"Perfect. So I'm going to be here on this table the whole time?"

"Yes. I'll leave you to change into your medical gown," I said. "Mrs. Steadhill?"

"I'll be out there waiting for you, dear," she said to her husband. He leaned towards her and gave her a small kiss on the corner of her lips. I noticed she turned her head slightly away as he kissed her.

"Right this way," I said, leading her back through the door to the waiting room. I closed the door behind us, then turned to find her staring at the glass globe full of brain tissue.

"Do you like it?" I asked.

"It's… it's beautiful," she said, bending to peer through the glass. Her dress lifted slightly and revealed a glimpse of her creamy thighs. In the mirrored wall, I could see her face intent on the sculpture. The concentration on her face was even more beautiful than the back view of her.

"Beautiful," I said, the word catching in my throat as I stepped forward. I would have her. She had walked straight into my trap, and now she was mine.

"What is it?"

"I'm sorry, what?"

"The sculpture," she said, still staring through the glass. The first person to ever notice. The first person ever to ask. "What is it?"

Sara

When the anesthesiologist touched my hand, I was deeply immersed in the part of Susan. I realized what Susan would do if an attractive young doctor started to flirt with her.

She would flirt right back.

"It's a plastic sculpture," Dr. Damore said. "Abstract art. I never understood it."

He was standing close to me, and I stood back up, shifting my weight closer to him. Our shoulders were almost touching, and I could feel the heat coming off of his body. As long as I didn't turn toward him, though, I could pretend as though I wasn't trying to touch him. Anyway, I could check him out in the mirror.

I wanted to, though. The one touch of his hand had sent thrills through me. And Susan's husband—my husband—was such a boring guy. Always at work. I deserved a little fun, didn't I? I had never felt so drawn to a person.

"The best art tells a story. But I think it's impossible to understand art like this," I said, tilting my head and studying the sculpture. The small pink-gray pieces of plastic seemed to connect together at points, like an organism growing out of its glass bowl. "It can mean anything. And whatever you think it means, the artist probably had a different meaning in mind."

"What do you think this artist meant?" the doctor asked. His voice was smooth, like honey. When I turned to face him, we were only a foot apart. My heart leapt in my chest.

"I think that whoever made this was trying to escape," I said, letting the bullshit flow off of my tongue. "He must have felt trapped."

"Trapped?"

"In a glass globe. See how it looks like an animal trying to get out?" I touched the top of the glass globe, letting my fingers stroke the glass the way I imagined wanting to stroke the doctor. I heard his breath and let my hand fall to my side.

"Like an animal in the zoo," he said. "Put there so that people could stare at it, watch it eat already-dead food and climb on concrete made to look like rocks."

"But it's an animal made of plastic. It's not real."

"Maybe nothing is real," he said.

I laughed, tilting my head back so that my hair fell and showed my exposed neck.

"Is that a message from your local plastic surgeon's office?"

"Hey, I only put them under. Whatever happens next is out of my hands."

I turned, and before the doctor could step back, I placed one hand lightly on his chest. Looking up, I fluttered my eyelashes softly and whispered to him.

"So if this is all fake, when do things turn real?"

Acting like I liked this guy was easy. Easier than any part I've ever played. He looked down at me with gold-brown eyes, and I could see his desire. I could feel it, like heat, radiating off of his body. His jawline, slightly accentuated with dark stubble. The slight flash of his teeth through his full lips. He wanted me, I knew it. And why wouldn't I want him? I could have anyone, after all. I was a CEO, a Hollywood wife, a millionaire. I could have anything I wanted.

"You're married," he murmured, looking at me

closely. "Aren't you?"

"Yes," I said. "We're such a perfect couple, too."

"Mrs. Steadhill…"

Before I could respond, the door to the operating room behind him opened. I let my hand fall away casually and turned back to the sculpture as though nothing had happened.

"I'm ready," Gary said, poking his head through the doorway. My ignorant husband.

"Wonderful," Dr. Damore said, smiling broadly. "Then let's get started. Mrs. Steadhill, would you like to sit in for the first part?"

"You mean, while you put him under?"

"Come on, honey," Gary said. "Come say goodnight, how about it?"

"Anything for you, darling," I said, my words dripping saccharine sweet. I followed Dr. Damore into the operating room.

My eyes darted to the view of L.A. as we walked in. Again, I had to stop myself from gaping out of the wall that was an entire window overlooking the valley. Probably Susan Steadhill saw views like that all the time, I told myself.

Dr. Damore helped Gary onto the operating room table and draped a sheet over his sides and lower body. Then he took out a syringe that was attached to the IV tubing. I turned away, wincing.

"Scared of needles?" Dr. Damore asked.

"Just a bit," I said. I wasn't sure if Susan was scared of needles, but I sure was. Gary hadn't given me much to go on for Susan's character, so I was making do with my own experiences. And, in my own experience, needles hurt like hell. I stared out at the Los Angeles landscape. The sun was lower in the sky, almost gone, and the lights were beginning to twinkle on all along the valley.

"Start counting down from one hundred," Dr. Damore said to Gary. I peeked back over my shoulder. The IV was in, and the doctor was depressing the plunger on the syringe.

"One hundred," Gary said. "Ninety-nine. Ninety-eight."

"Good. Keep counting."

Dr. Damore stepped away from the operating table.

"Ninety-seven. Ninety-six."

"Nice view, isn't it?" the anesthesiologist said, coming close to me. "Soon your husband will be out. I'll monitor him closely." Behind us, I could hear Gary still counting down, his voice getting groggy.

"Ninety-five."

"Good," I said, casting my eyes down. The cars below reflected flashes of sunlight. "I trust you with his life."

Was that too dramatic? I hoped that wasn't too dramatic. But I felt dramatic.

"Ninety-four. Ninety... ninety-three." His voice was fading.

"I'll take good care of him," Dr. Damore said.

"I have no doubt."

"I'll take good care of you, too," Dr. Damore whispered.

I turned in shock that he would make such a bold statement. The doctor was standing so close to me that I could feel his breath. I looked past him, to where Gary was lying on the table. His eyes were closed, and a line of drool ran from one corner of his mouth as he snored. My heart beat faster. What was I doing, playing with fire? I was supposed to be pretending like our marriage was alright. Suddenly I felt a flash of worry. I had gone too far with acting. I shouldn't be Susan. I should be a better version of Susan.

"Where's the surgeon?" I asked.

"Don't worry about him," Dr. Damore said. He reached out and touched my cheek, tilting my chin upward.

Then he kissed me, and I fell against his chest as he pulled me into the embrace. His lips were soft, and the stubble on his chin grazed mine. His arms circled around me, and I felt as though I was being lifted up. Like I was floating. Heat thrummed through my body and I felt myself clench with desire, despite myself. Oh, Lord, he knew how to kiss. His lips pulled and pushed in equal measure, and my body responded like a candle flame responding to wind, instantly letting him take me where he wanted to go.

His mouth moved down my chin, his lips against my neck now. Wherever he kissed me, my skin burned with delight. I felt dizzy; the world outside was spinning.

"Dr. Damore," I murmured, putting my hand on his chest. His arms were locked around me, his muscles taut. I pushed away slightly, but he didn't react at all. "Please."

"So beautiful," he said, his mouth still against my neck.

"Hey," I said, struggling now to push away. His arms, though, were like a vise around me. I couldn't get out. "Hey, don't... come on. I can't... we can't do this."

"Such a shame," he murmured. His body pressed against mine, and I could feel his hardness against me. Then he twisted my arm behind my back in one motion. I gasped as his other hand came up, holding a syringe. My heart pounded. What was going on? What was he doing? I squirmed in his arms but he had me pinned tightly against him. I couldn't even move.

"Hey!" I cried. "Wait! Stop!"

"I'm sorry, dear Mrs. Steadhill," he said, and then I felt a pinch on the side of my neck. Then, nothing.

CHAPTER EIGHT

Rien

Mrs. Steadhill. Not the most faithful of wives. I wouldn't kill a woman for that, not alone. But it made me feel a bit better about injecting her with a sedative.

Unlike her husband, she was out instantly. The sedative I gave her was fast-acting and fast to wear off. She would be awake again in a minute, probably about the same time as her husband. Just in time to watch him die. For now, though, she was my sleeping beauty.

She slumped into my arms, her head lolling as the sedative took over. I laid her on the floor and pulled the second operating table alongside her husband's before picking her back up in my arms.

Her curves felt so tender under my hands as I carried her over to the operating table. I placed her gently on the table and left her there, then moved over to her husband and pulled his straps tight. One over his head. Two straps for each leg and arm. Another across the pelvis that would keep him from twisting or bucking when I operated. Then I strapped her down, being a bit more gentle. I caressed her hip as I pulled the strap across it, making sure to adjust the sheet so she would be comfortable when she woke up. I straightened out her hair on the pillow before adjusting the strap across her brow line. Then I changed my mind. She would need to move her head so that she could see her husband while I worked. I would strap her head down later, and gag her then too. I checked her eyes for dilation. One unfocused pupil stared up at me.

Strange. I bent down to see what it was, and realized that she was wearing contacts. Carefully, I slid the contact lens to the side of her eye. So. She had green eyes, not blue. If the eyes were windows to the soul, hers were fake. All fake. I slid the contact lens back in.

Normally that would disgust me, but I felt none of my usual disdain as I looked down at her. I didn't know what it was about her that drew me to her. Perhaps it was that she had noticed my sculpture. Was I that vain?

Yes, maybe I was.

She stirred a little, a soft gasp escaping her lips. I smiled. She would be awake soon enough. It was time to wake up hubby and get started with the surgery. Turning back to him, I inserted the adrenaline injection into the IV. Then I tied the gag around his mouth. I didn't like to gag unconscious patients—they tended to choke to death—but he was on his way out of sleep. Soon his breathing grew faster and his eyes opened.

"Hello," I said, looking down at my victim. "Change of plans, Mr. Steadhill. I'll be your surgeon today."

Sara

"*MMMMM!*"

Everything was warm and fuzzy. The way it felt after I'd had two too many glasses of wine with dinner. The lights overhead were bright, though, and I tried to raise my hand to cover my eyes. It wouldn't move; there was something holding it down.

"*MMMMHHHMMM!*"

That noise. What was that noise?

I blinked and saw fuzzy white dots floating in my vision. Everything was white. Beautiful. I thought I might have died and gone to heaven.

"*MMMMM*!"

That noise again. I blinked hard. It was coming from my left. My muscles felt heavy, weighted down. I let my head fall to the side. Staring back at me was something out of *Nightmare on Elm Street*, a monster with a face of blood. It made the noise again and I realized that it was Gary.

I screamed.

The whole side of Gary's face had been peeled back, revealing all of the muscles and tendons of his cheeks. The only thing that had been left alone, it seemed, was his eye, and that same eye now turned to lock on mine, fixing me with a dead gaze that had no eyelid.

I screamed again and tried to shove myself away, but nothing happened. My arms and legs wouldn't move. I twisted my body to try to get away, but I realized that there was something tying me down to the bed I was lying on.

Then I saw him.

It was the anesthesiologist. He had taken off his surgical cap, and his dark hair fell in front of his eyes as he bent over the top of the table I was tied to.

"Help me!" I cried. "Dr. Damore, help!"

My mind was slow, muddled, and the walls of the room spun around me like a carousel. What had happened? He had kissed me, and then—

Oh, shit.

My eyes widened as the pieces fell into place. He had stuck me with a needle. It was him.

"I'll help you," he said. "You and your husband both."

My husband? Oh, right. I was supposed to be Susan. I blinked again.

"But please, call me Rien," he continued. "Now that we're getting to know each other better."

"Rien?" I echoed dumbly. Was I awake, or still dreaming? A thought spiraled through my mind as I looked wildly around the spinning room. Maybe this was still part of the role. Maybe I was on a prank show right now.

"This isn't real, is it?" I asked.

"Real? Nothing is real. Isn't that what you were telling me before?"

"No, but really. I mean..." I trailed off. If this was a show, then I didn't want to break character. I would lose the cash. On the other hand, he had stuck me with a needle! It couldn't be a show. Could it? God, what was happening to me? I swallowed and tried to clear my focus.

Next to me, Gary squealed. I darted a glance his way. Blood pooled onto the sheet, and his face was *peeled off of his head*. Okay. Right. Not a show. Definitely not a show. I looked back at the doctor. Rien. Even though the walls were still blurry, his eyes were sharply focused.

On me.

"Holy shit. This is real."

"Real? Maybe. What does real mean? You're both living a lie already. Fake people, fake lives. And now you want to go start fresh somewhere else." Rien, if that was really his name, twirled a scalpel in his fingers. I stared at the silver blade flashing in the light. It was hypnotizing.

"This is a mistake," I stammered. My tongue felt thick in my mouth as I talked. I couldn't get my head clear, and the room hadn't decided to stay still yet.

"I agree, you've made quite a few mistakes if you ended up here," he said. Next to me, Gary was still making that horrible wet noise behind his gag.

"No, you don't understand. I'm not Mrs. Steadhill. You've got the wrong person."

"Really? Is that so?"

"I'm serious!" I said, my voice rising in panic. The room was getting more steady now—the adrenaline of my panic seemed to be slapping my senses back into focus. It was still hard to breathe. "I'm not married to him!"

"Funny, because when we were out in the waiting room you told me you were married to him. Not that your marriage seems that stable—"

"I was lying! I was acting! I'm an act— *mmmmmmmm!*"

Without warning, he shoved a ball of cotton gauze into my mouth.

My tongue went suddenly dry, all the moisture soaked up the cotton, and I gagged. Whatever he had stuck me with was still in my system, and I felt my throat muscles spasming as I tried to push the cotton out of my mouth with my tongue. Rien slapped medical tape across my mouth, pressing the ends down on my cheeks, to hold it in. Tears burned my eyes.

"Maybe your husband can help you figure out this situation, Susan," he said.

I shook my head. *I'm not Susan!*

"Would you like to say something to your loving wife, Mr. Steadhill? Before I get started on her?"

Panic burned at my nerves. *Holy shit, holy shit, holy shit.* He was going to cut my face off, too. He was a crazy killer pretending to be a plastic surgeon, and Gary had walked us both right into his house. A low whimper rose from my throat involuntarily. What was I doing here? What was happening?

Rien leaned over and ripped off Gary's taped gag. I was pretty sure part of Gary's lips went with it, because he screamed at the top of his lungs. Then Rien waved the scalpel over his face, and he stopped screaming. I could see the blood vessels in his face throbbing as he held back the scream. That terrified me more than anything else.

"You remember how we started," Rien said. Gary nodded. "Alright. Now, then."

"It's a mistake," Gary said. His voice was ragged and wet, and when he talked I could see his cheek muscles contracting along his jawline. "I'm part of the witness protection program. With the FBI."

What? Behind the gag, I shrieked. What the hell was he talking about? *FBI?* He had lied to me, too! This was insane. Absolutely insane.

"We had a police escort here," Gary continued. The corner of his mouth, or what was left of it, leaked blood. He sounded calm, calmer than I would have been if someone had cut up half of my face and peeled it off like a fruit rollup. "Then I was going to go straight to the airport and fly to Brazil under a new alias."

His breathing was hard, labored, the words forced. His bare eye rolled toward me, then back to Rien. A shudder ran down my spine.

"Susan was going to come join me a week later, after her surgery."

I shook my head wildly. *No! I'm not Susan!*

"So you see, this must all be a misunderstanding," Gary said.

"Misunderstanding. Hmm," the doctor said. He glanced over at me, then back to Gary. Lifting the scalpel, he placed the point directly on Gary's chest.

"Please! It's true! The police are coming back for us in a few hours!"

The muscle above his eyeball jumped, and I realized that he was trying to blink with an eyelid that wasn't attached to him anymore. Bile rose in my throat, and I held back my retching. If I threw up, I'd choke to death on it.

"Are they? Tell me, Mr. Steadhill, what crimes did

you get away with when you made your deal with the FBI?"

The doctor—Rien—stood very still, his hand poised with the scalpel on Gary's chest.

"I—I'm not a criminal," Gary stammered.

The scalpel pressed down and I could see blood leaking from both sides. Gary screamed aloud.

"Stop! Stop! *Please stop!*"

"Only if you tell me the truth. Once again, then. What crimes were you convicted of before you squealed on someone else?"

"Aghhh! Stop! Alright! I'll tell you! Cor—corporate espionage. We sent people in to other companies. Sabotaged factories."

I flailed my head from side to side. Why did he keep saying we? *I* didn't do any of this shit!

"What else?"

"Nothing."

"What else?" The scalpel slid down his chest, and I could hear the slicing noise as the skin tore under the blade.

"AHHHHHH! Mmm—manslaughter. Criminal negligence." His teeth were chattering, and I could see his jawbone through the blood.

I clenched my eyes shut. Dear God, who was this man?

"How many deaths were you responsible for, the both of you?"

I opened my eyes then and stared at Rien, locking eyes with him. I shook my head slowly from one side to the other. No. I didn't kill anyone. He stared back at me with a curious expression on his face, then tilted his head towards Gary.

"Mr. Steadhill?"

"Two hundred sixty. But it wasn't our fault. The sabotage went wrong! It was a mistake—"

"Yes," Rien said. "A mistake. There seem to be lots of mistakes around here."

He stepped back and walked around to the foot of the operating table.

"Let me tell you one other mistake you made, Mr. Steadhill. You didn't tell anyone in your life that you were going into the witness protection program, did you? No, of course you didn't. That's part of the witness protection program."

Gary's teeth chattered more. Pus leaked from below his reddened eye.

"And the United States of America, in their generosity, decided to give you a new life in another country. They told you to come to me for a new face, and then you would fly to Brazil for a new life. Is that right? They told you everything would be taken care of, didn't they?"

A chill swept over my body as I realized what Rien was saying. He glanced over my way as though he could read my thoughts.

"Unfortunately for you and your wife, Mr. Steadhill, the U.S. government doesn't really care that much for corporate saboteurs, especially those who get innocent citizens killed."

"We gave them information," Gary said. "They said—"

"They said whatever they needed to say to get you here. Sorry to tell you that your car won't be coming back for you this evening. The United States has washed its hands of you, Mr. Steadhill. They have sent you on a snipe hunt. There are no plane tickets to Brazil. There is no new identity for you or your wife."

"But—but—"

"There's only me. Understand that? And now... you're mine."

CHAPTER NINE

Rien

It was time to start carving up this couple. And with nobody else on my schedule, I could take my time and enjoy it.

Mrs. Steadhill was screaming behind her gag, her body twisting against the straps. I would definitely have to tie her neck down or risk being sloppy. But first I'd deal with her husband.

I picked up the cotton to stuff it in Mr. Steadhill's mouth again.

"Wait! She isn't my wife," he said, rasping air.

I paused. The nagging feeling that I had gotten when the couple walked in was back. I had assumed that she had been lying, but a worry itched at my mind.

"She's an actress," he continued. "She—"

I stuffed the gag in his mouth. He choked as I taped it back up, shrieking as the tape touched his musculature on the exposed part of his face.

"An actress?"

I looked over at the woman. She nodded frantically, her eyes wide.

"I can tell you want to talk," I said. "But I've found that when I let people talk to me, they lie. Are you going to lie?"

She shook her head. Tears leaked out of the corners of her eyes. A twist of unease made its way into my stomach as I looked at her. If she really was innocent, I couldn't kill her. But I couldn't let her go. She was a witness.

If she was innocent, that is.

"Then we'll talk," I said, deciding quickly. "In another room. I don't trust the two of you together."

I went over to the medical cabinet and pulled out another hypodermic, then brought it over to the woman. She looked at the needle with terror in her eyes and looked away as I injected her.

"You are scared of needles, aren't you?"

She nodded, her eyes clenched shut.

"Oh, that is such a shame. It would have been *so* much fun to torture you."

I undid the strap around one of her arms. She opened her eyes and stared down at what I was doing. I raised her arm and let it drop. It fell limply to the table. Excellent. She frowned, looking down at her arm as though willing it to move.

"Paralyzed. Yes," I said, undoing the rest of the straps. "You're not going anywhere without me."

I slid my arms underneath her and picked her up. Her head lolled against my chest, the cotton gag still stuffed in her mouth. She whimpered.

"Goodbye, Mr. Steadhill," I said. "You've been granted a short reprieve. I'll be back later."

The man moaned, but I was already carrying my new toy across the room. With my elbow, I pressed the hidden button on the side of the medical cabinet. The back wall opened up and I carried her through the secret doorway.

Sara

I couldn't move my arms or legs. I thought I must be dreaming. It's only in dreams you can't move. Those nightmares where you try to run, but your muscles don't work, and you're frozen in place. Trying to get away from the boogie monster.

Now the monster had me in his arms.

The doctor picked me up easily, as though I was a small child he was carrying in his arms. He paused at the back of the operating room, shifting my weight in his arms. Then the back wall of the operating room *opened* and we stepped into another room. A dark room. The door closed behind us and I could barely see the sliver of light coming from the other room.

My eyes were still adjusting as he put me down on something soft. A couch. I felt his hands peel off the tape on my gag. Then the wet cotton was gone and I could *breathe*. I gasped air, sucking in deep breaths.

"Easy, now," he said. "You'll hyperventilate if you breathe too fast." His voice was gentle. *A gentle killer*, I thought. I must be going crazy.

He walked over and turned on the light, and then I could see where I was.

Shelves of books surrounded me on all sides that I could see. There was a single leather couch in the middle of the room, and a small endtable with a lamp. The doctor was standing next to the lamp. His hand fell down to his side. I tried to move my lips. My jaw wouldn't move, but I could form the words I wanted to, even if they sounded a bit mumbled.

"Doctor... doctor Damore—"

"Rien. Please. Call me Rien."

He walked over to where I was lying down and knelt beside me. I wanted to run, oh God, I wanted to run. The look in his eyes was back, the look of a predator. It made me think of a book I had read when I was a kid, called *Watership Down*. The book was about rabbits, and they had a word for the feeling I was experiencing right now. The feeling that something so dangerous is looking at you that you can't move. You're so scared that every muscle freezes, and you can't even run away. They called it *going tharn.*

I was going tharn right then. I didn't know what to say, or if anything I said would matter. I couldn't even move when he took my hand and held it in both of his.

"I've given you something that causes temporary paralysis. So you can't run away. Do you understand?"

"Yes," I whispered.

One of his hands moved up, stroking my arm. The touch sent a shiver through my body, only my body couldn't shiver anymore.

"You can still feel this, can't you? You can feel my hand?"

"Y—yes," I said.

"Good. I'm glad you can still feel things."

"Rien. Please. Listen to me. I'm not Mrs. Steadhill."

"No, you're not, are you?" Rien said. His voice sounded absentminded, as though he was far away. His hand still caressed my arm slowly, sending those slow thrills through my body. He cupped my elbow for a moment, his warm palm holding me as though measuring something, then went back to stroking. His hand moved from my fingers up my forearm, trailing up to where my navy dress stopped at the shoulder. Susan's navy dress.

"Please," I said. "I don't know who that man is out there, but I'm not married to him. He hired me as an actress. My name is Sara. Sara Everett. I hadn't even met that man before today!"

"Is that right?"

I breathed in deeply. My panic receded a bit, now that I wasn't lying next to a half-dissected Gary. I tried to think clearly.

"He hired me to act like his wife."

"Is that what you were doing when you flirted with

me?"

I stared up at Rien's eyes. In the dim light, his irises looked like tigereye. Deep brown with a ribbon of gold floating within. His expression was blank even as his hand kept caressing my arm. One long stroke after another. In a way, it was soothing.

"I was playing the part."

"Did the part call for kissing someone other than your husband?"

"You were the one who kissed me!" I cried.

"You didn't stop me."

"I tried to. I did. Anyway, she thought you were attractive."

"She?"

"Susan. My character," I stammered. "That is, I thought she would think you were attractive. I wanted it to be realistic. He told me that his wife flirted with lots of other men."

"That's what he told you?"

"Yes."

"So you were only playing a part."

"Yes." I breathed out a sigh. "So you see, I'm not the person you want to kill."

"No," he agreed. "I can't kill you."

I almost cried with relief. He wasn't going to kill me. He understood. This was all a mistake.

"Thank you," I said. "Thank you. I just want this to be over."

"Oh, it's not over," he said.

"I—what?"

"This isn't over at all," he said. He raised one hand to my face and caressed my cheek.

"It's not over," he repeated. "Not for you, anyway."

"You said you wouldn't kill me," I said. Panic choked my throat. "You said—"

"I won't kill you," Rien said. "But I can't let you

go."

CHAPTER TEN

Rien

She looked up at me with such horror that I almost laughed. Oh, yes, she was a problem. A terribly sticky problem. But I always dealt with problems. I didn't doubt my ability to figure out how to deal with this particular problem.

In the meantime, I had a new toy to play with.

"I'm sorry. Is the paralysis still working correctly? You can feel my hands, right?" I touched her temple, rubbing in a slow circle.

She nodded.

"Y—yes. I can feel everything."

"You are a beautiful young woman, Sara," I said. My hand moved alongside her jawline, memorizing the softness of her skin. Her eyes followed my fingers as they moved. "A very interesting young woman. An aspiring actress. Trying to get your big break, yes? And somehow you managed to end up here."

"What are you doing?" she asked. Her voice trembled.

"Don't worry," I said. "I won't kill you."

"That's not what I asked."

I smiled.

"You know something, Sara?"

"Let me go," she whispered. In her eyes I could tell she was beginning to understand that she wasn't getting out of this room.

"I've never made anyone feel good before. I always

torture them."

She stared at me wordlessly. I ran my fingers through her hair, spreading the long dark locks over the couch. Her hair was the same shade of brown as the leather.

"Like your fake husband in the other room there," I said. "I woke him up before beginning to cut. Then I cut right along the hairline as he screamed and screamed. You didn't wake up. I peeled his skin back with forceps as he screamed."

Her eyes watered, and I could see fear creeping into her.

"He deserved every last little bit of torture," I said. "And that wasn't even the last bit! Oh, no. That was only the beginning. He's still alive."

A tear ran down her cheek. I reached down and wiped it away with my thumb.

"Don't worry, beautiful Sara. You're not like him, are you?"

She shook her head tightly, the tears starting to come heavily now.

"Please—"

"Don't ask me again to let you go. I won't. But I won't torture you like that, either. Not if you're not a bad person. You're not a bad person, are you?"

"No." Her voice was a crack in the dark air of the library.

"Then I won't hurt you. But you know something, Sara? It's true. I've never made anyone feel good— really *good*—before."

My hands moved slowly behind her back to unclasp her dress.

"You can feel everything?" I asked.

"Rien—"

"Good. Then this should be very, *very* fun."

Sara

I gaped as Rien's hands moved around underneath my back. I hadn't lied—I could feel every touch of his.

"What are you doing?" I asked.

"Having a bit of fun."

He unzipped the back of my dress. His hands moved up and slid my shoulder straps down.

"No," I said, unwilling to believe that this was happening. "No. Rien."

He leaned forward and kissed me on my bare neck. His lips burned my skin with heat. Despite myself, I felt my body respond to his touch. His hand moved down over my breasts, my stomach, and came to rest on my hip. He clasped me there and kissed me lightly on the underside of my chin.

"You're the only one who's ever commented on my sculpture," he said. His mouth was right next to my ear. "Did you know that? Most people ignore it. I'm glad you can appreciate art, even if you didn't understand what I meant by it."

"What... what—"

"You thought I felt trapped, yes? Trapped in the glass globe. But I am the artist. I'm not trapped anywhere. You're the one who's trapped."

"Rien, please—"

"Trapped here with me."

His hand moved down and pulled the hem of my dress up. I gasped as he slid his hand underneath and pressed his fingers against my panties. A ferocious aching heat tore through my body at his touch down there. I wanted to twist away from him, but I couldn't move. Worst of all, as his fingers began to slide up, I felt a terrible need for more, more pressure.

"Don't—"

"No? You don't want this?" He pulled his hand away, and a whimper escaped my throat involuntarily at the sudden departure.

He smiled. The gold in his eyes shone brightly.

"Don't lie to me, Sara. Liars get punished. And you know what my kind of punishment is like."

I made a choking cry as I looked away. This wasn't me. I wasn't here. This was only a character, I thought. I could get through this, as long as it was pretend.

Only pretend.

"This is new to me, too, Sara," he whispered. "I've never made anyone feel... good like this before."

He put his fingers back where they had been, stroking me through the fabric. I held back a moan. The strokes were setting my body afire, the spark of desire kindling an ache between my thighs that his fingers did nothing to relieve. His other hand grasped the top of my dress and pulled it down, exposing my breasts.

"Rien—"

"Hush. I know what you want. I can tell from your breath."

I bit down on my tongue as he bent over and kissed the tip of my nipple. The touch would have made my back arch against the couch, if my muscles worked. Tears burned the backs of my eyes, but this time they were tears of frustration.

His tongue came out and licked me, curving around my nipple. His dark hair tickled my skin. I could feel everything, yes—the roughness of stubble on his chin on the underside of my breast, the softness of his hot tongue. And his lips—

"Oh!" I cried aloud as he sealed his lips around my nipple and sucked hard. The fire in my body roared to new heights. The hand under my dress slid under my panties. I nearly screamed as his fingers explored my folds.

"God, you're wet," he whispered. His breath chilled my nipple, making it harden. "You must want me so badly."

No. I didn't want this. I didn't want this. I didn't want—

"*Ohhhh!*" I moaned. He had plunged his fingers into me, and my body clenched around him. I wanted to buck against his hand, I wanted him to thrust his fingers deep into me, again, again, again...

What was I thinking? What was I feeling? My body was a traitor, making me ache for this man, this killer, this criminal who would think nothing of opening me up. But oh, lord, when his fingers touched me inside, all I could think of was him opening me up in a different way, doing it again, harder, faster...

Instead, he slid his fingers out slowly. The agony was unbearable, and I groaned. My panties were soaked now; I could feel the wet fabric against my skin. I needed him inside of me again, needed his touch. *This!* This was everything I had wanted. His hands possessed some magic that shuddered me down to the core. His eyes stared at me so open and desiring. He was real. His desire was real. And he wanted me.

"Tell me what you want, Sara," he murmured. His lips traced a circle around my breast. I blinked back my tears. I would not give in to him, no, not now. I would be strong. I would get through this.

Without warning, he sucked my nipple hard. A jolt of pain shot through my body, and I cried aloud. He released my nipple, and the relief washed through my body, along with a terrible desire for more. My pulse quickened.

"Then I suppose I'll have to read you," he said, his whisper. "Try not to fake it too much. Otherwise, how will I know what you want?"

"I don't... I don't want—"

"No. No, of course you don't."

His fingers went back to stroking me on either side, not putting any pressure where I needed it most. The hollow ache of my core was so needy that I wanted to scream. How could my body be so responsive to this man? He was a crazy person, certifiably insane. A murderer. And yet, when his finger grazed my swollen sex, I nearly cried with delight.

His mouth moved to my other nipple, leaving the first one aching and sore. And still his fingers stroked, stroked, everywhere except where I needed. As his teeth ran across my breast, I shivered in anticipation.

What kind of a person was I, that this man could make me need him so much?

He pulled his hand back from underneath my dress, and I nearly sobbed with frustration. I couldn't let him see how much I wanted release. I couldn't let him see what heights he had brought me to.

With the hand that had been stroking me, he now reached up to my exposed breast. With one nipple in his mouth, he pinched the other with his thumb and finger. A cry escaped my throat as the pinch sent a searing burn through my chest. His fingers were still wet with my juices, and the pinch turned into a slick caress over my erect nipple.

"Am I hurting you? Please tell me if I am so I can ignore you."

"Rien—"

He twisted my nipple hard, and I screamed, a short scream that went nowhere in the library, sucked up by the pages of the books that surrounded us.

"Pain and pleasure aren't really different, are they?" he asked. "Like flipping your pillow over in the middle of the night. One side warm, one cold. You must have one before the other feels good again."

He twisted again, and instead of screaming, I drew a breath inside of me, trying desperately to retreat from my body. I was not there. I was not feeling anything. This wasn't me. I was a character again. I felt nothing, and nothing hurt. I would not be affected by Rien. He had no power over me.

But then he bent his head and took my hurt nipple into his mouth and I was pulled back into my body again. His tongue softened on my breast, caressing, and I bit back a moan of pleasure. Yes, he had power. He could make me want him, despite everything.

"I said I wouldn't hurt you, Sara, but I can't help myself." His hand moved down and rested on my stomach. Such a small, intimate gesture. It made nausea twist through me. The way he held me, stroked me—it was as though I was his possession. His toy. And he was doing whatever he wanted with me, including toying with my emotions.

I closed my eyes and tried to remember him with the scalpel. Him torturing Gary on the operating room table. I tried to remember all of the blood. If I could hold onto these images, I could fight back against this feeling that threatened to take my whole body over.

He sucked in air, teeth grazing my nipple, and I shivered with the chill of air moving across my aching sensitive skin.

"I hope you're enjoying this, Sara," he said. "I don't want any harm to come to you. Permanent harm, that is. But it's been so long since I've had... fun like this. It's hard to find the right kind of person. The kind of person who would enjoy it."

I opened my eyes. He was leaning over me, looking straight into my face. His hair was dark, but his eyes were golden. So warm that I wanted to reach out to him for help. *Save me from yourself.*

I wanted to tell him no, that I wasn't that kind of

person. The kind of person who would enjoy this: being paralyzed, brought to dangle dangerously over a torturous edge of pleasure. But that wouldn't be true. As much as I outwardly reviled him, my skin ached for his touch.

Under his fingers, my body *hummed*.

Still looking deep into my eyes, Rien slid his hand back down under my panties. I sucked in air and didn't scream as his fingers moved alongside my entrance, his hot needful fingertips probing, stroking, caressing my folds. My heart pounded in my ears, thrumming like music.

"Rien..."

He said nothing, only leaned forward. His lips were inches from mine. His eyes fixed mine, and I thought again of the rabbits in that book. How, when they had come face to face with a predator, they froze and could not move. Even if I had not been sedated, I don't think I could have moved an inch.

Again his fingers slid into me, thick and slow. I gasped as he filled me, stretching my opening slowly, slowly, so slowly that my eyes burned with tears of frustration.

"Rien."

His lips moved slightly, but I could not make out his words. His fingers slid out, then back again, again slowly. I moaned. Forgotten were all of my promises to myself. I could not keep myself from wanting this, no, not when his fingers stretched me and tortured me with the thought of ecstasy just over the edge. I would fall, he would make me fall. My body ached to arch against his fingers, but I had no control over any muscles down there and I had to wait.

Wait for him.

"Please, Rien," I murmured, staring up into his eyes. I could not read his face; he was hidden from me. His fingers slid in and out faster, though, and I cried out loud as his thumb grazed my swollen, aching clit.

"*Yes.*" I said. I could feel the end coming. I felt my body rising up inside as his rhythm matched exactly what I would have chosen, had I been able to move. His fingers thrust into me over and over, his thumb brushing me again and sending another gasp shuddering through my body. I was close. *So close.*

The light in the room seemed to flicker and dim, but that was only my eyelashes fluttering as I felt the pressure inside of me build and come to a head.

"*Harder,*" I whispered, "*harder, oh please, harder,*" and clenched my eyes shut, waiting for my release.

Then his fingers slid out and he was gone.

Gone?

My body ached for fingers that no longer touched me. I opened my eyes, my breath ragged in my throat, staring up at him in disbelief. My body clenched, clenched at nothing. He was gone, and I felt utterly hollow. His face was implacable, totally unreadable. He didn't frown, or scowl.

"Rien," I gasped. "Please don't... don't stop..."

He smiled as he leaned back, away from me, and raised his hand between us. His fingers glistened in the light. As I watched, he licked my juices off of his hand, one finger at a time.

I moaned. My body was wracked with a need that overpowered all rational thought.

"That's enough playtime for now. You're an excellent actress, Sara. I almost believed you there, at the end."

Anger flooded me. I hated him for bringing me here. I hated him for the pain and the pleasure, for offering me release and tearing it away at the last moment. Most of all, I hated him for not believing me.

"You can't..." I whimpered, hating too the sound of

my own voice, whiny and clinging. "Please. You can't stop. I'm so close."

"You're not close to anything," Rien said. "I can see it in your eyes. You're still holding on to whatever ideas you had of me before. You're not here. You're somewhere else."

"I'm not," I cried angrily. "I swear…"

"Next time," he said, standing up, "I want you to keep your eyes open. The whole time. You understand? Or I'll never take you any further."

He put his hands in his pockets and stood there casually, waiting for my reply. My whole body, every cell, clamored for touch, and now he was pulling away. Taunting me. Teasing me. Making me want something and then taking it away. I hated him for it.

"Fuck you," I hissed.

He smiled then. I hated him even more for smiling because he was so beautiful when he smiled. A beautiful face that hid a monster behind it.

"I like you, Sara," he said, his smile twinkling in his eyes. "I think we'll have a lot of fun together. You won't have very much fun right now, I suppose. You probably won't be able to move for another hour."

A cry choked in my throat. An hour? I had to wait an hour before I could move. An hour before I could touch myself and get rid of this awful ache. It seemed impossible.

"Or I could bring you around sooner and strap you back down on the operating table in the other room. I'm heading there now, actually. If you'd like to join Mr. Steadhill and see what *real* torture is, I'm sure I could arrange it."

"No," I whispered.

"Good. Then I'll see you later, my dear Sara." He bent down and kissed my forehead—and God, my body thrummed another ache as his lips touched my skin—

and left the room. I lay on the couch, unable to move, unable to do anything but think about the monster who had captured me and how awfully, terribly much I wanted to feel his touch again.

CHAPTER ELEVEN

Rien

What a wonderful plaything. It was like learning a new instrument when I touched her.

I hummed as I passed through the secret bookcase door, the wall sliding back into place behind me. On the operating room table, Mr. Steadhill was still breathing heavily. I turned on the music, a light classical quartet piece by someone I didn't know. Baroque, maybe. The strings trilled their melodies in the air.

I snapped on my gloves. Pleasure first, then pain. I enjoyed inflicting pleasure on the girl, but pain was my first love. Now, I picked up an eyedropper of silver nitrate and pulled up a stool next to the operating room table. Mr. Steadhill was asleep, but he would not be asleep for long. Raising the silver nitrate above the bare half of his face, I let the liquid drop onto his exposed tissue.

He woke with a jerk, his body twisting on the table. The screams from behind his gag did not go well with the music, and I frowned, reminding myself to go back to the linen-knotted gag instead of cotton. _Drip, drip, drip_ went the eyedropper.

I remembered when my parents had forced me to learn the cello. All of their friends had children who could play the piano or the violin. My mother didn't love cello music, but she loved the idea of cello music. And she loved the idea of having a son who could play such an instrument. What a thing to brag about!

At first I'd hated it, but then I started to practice alone in my room. When I took up the cello and set it in front of me, cradled between my knees, I realized that I liked it. I liked the way my fingers curled around the neck. I liked the way I could scrape the bow across the strings. The low notes would vibrate the wood so that my whole body trembled along with it. The notes would run through me like waves of water.

Once my mother realized I loved the cello, she sold it and bought a grand piano instead. I never played another note.

Drip, drip, drip. The silver nitrate would cauterize the facial wounds that were already becoming infected. Although my operating room was sterile, the air was not. I thought back to my medical school lessons. One of the first scientific experiments to prove that infections could move through air was by deliberately infecting patients. It was something that my professors had called inhumane. Back then, doctors would put an infected patient next to an uninfected one. The only thing between them was a gauze membrane. They did not touch, but the infection would spread from one patient to another. Then they knew that the disease passed through air as easily as through bodily contact.

Was that inhumane? The knowledge of these diseases must have saved thousands of lives afterwards. I couldn't judge these early doctors for their actions. They thought that what they were doing was for the best.

"What I am doing is for the best," I said, dripping the silver nitrate onto Mr. Steadhill's face. He screamed and screamed and did not understand. His muscles twitched under the drips of the concentrated liquid. His eye was glazed over, reddened. I would have sprayed it with saline, but he really didn't need his sight in both eyes. Instead, I dripped silver nitrate onto the eye.

Oh, how he howled! It was a glorious sound, even

muffled.

"Now you'll live for longer," I said, patting Mr. Steadhill on the shoulder. "I know that might not be what you want, but it's for the best."

The music played on and I cleaned up, putting back the silver nitrate and storing the extra operating table off to the side. I did not think Sara would need to come back into this room. I would keep her in the library.

Yes, that would work. I whistled as I washed my hands in the sink, happy to have part of the plan figured out. Mr. Steadhill would die soon; I would keep him around for another couple of days. I had an idea of how to use him, but the idea wasn't completely clear in my mind. Still, I was happy to have him around to play with, especially since I didn't have any other clients this week. Perhaps he would offer to pay me for his release.

And Sara. *Sara.* She was a new instrument to learn. I understood only a tiny sliver of her so far, but I was certain I would know more. I would get better. She was unfamiliar to me now, but I would uncover the desires that ran through her, all of the nuances of what she wanted from my fingers and lips. She was new, and innocent, and although I did not know if she would stay, for now I would keep her and discover more about her. Soon, I would tease out all of her secrets.

Soon, I would make her body sing.

Sara

My fingers moved first, twitching at my side. Once I saw them move, I wiggled my toes. The effect of whatever he used to paralyze me was wearing off quickly. Soon I was able to lift my entire right arm. I pulled my dress down, pulled the straps back up. I used my one good arm to prop myself up on the couch. I still ached for release, but reconnaissance was more important right now. I suppressed my body's aching and looked around.

The library wasn't very big. Behind the couch was a wall filled entirely with shelves. I tried to figure out where the opening was. We had come through that wall, I was sure of it, but I couldn't tell which part of the bookcase was the doorway. Maybe there was a hidden switch or something. There had been a switch from the other side, I remembered, but from this side?

In the corner was a small end table. A stained glass lamp rested on top of it, casting a dim colored light over the room. And there was another door, a real door this time, that led to another part of the house that I hadn't seen.

I'd walked into this house as Susan, but now I was another character. As I looked around, trying to find a way to escape, I settled into my new character. It was a stereotype, sure, but one that I'd seen acted out a million times in movies. The Survivor. The survivor was a strong woman. She didn't let anything get in the way of her goal.

What was her goal? Easy. *Escape.* By any means possible.

I couldn't do this by myself. I couldn't do this as Sara. But I could do it as the survivor. That's who I would be, I decided. From here on out. I would be smart and resourceful. I would look for chances to get out. I would take those chances. And I wouldn't let him know that I was trying to leave.

The doorknob turned. Startled, I fell back onto the couch. I didn't want him to guess that the paralysis was wearing off. Secret. That's what the survivor was. She never let any information slip that could possibly be useful. Already, her presence inside of me made me a little bit more confident. Bold. If I couldn't figure out how to get out of here, then she would.

Rien came in through the oak door carrying a tray. I peered over and saw a glimpse of a hallway through the door opening before it shut behind him.

"Dinnertime," he said as he approached the couch. He set the tray down on the floor. It smelled delicious, a warm spicy tomato smell and my stomach growled. I didn't want to eat anything that he had made me, though. Eating would admit defeat, wouldn't it? I didn't want to admit to him or to myself that I was a hostage here. Survivors didn't admit defeat.

He shifted my body over so that there was room for him on the couch. One of the two decorative pillows fell to the floor. Gently, he put the pillow behind my neck and propped my head on it. I winced as his fingers brushed against my cheek, thinking about what had happened before. Thinking about what he had done to me already. Would he touch me again?

Would I want him to?

He picked up the bowl and offered me a spoonful. I looked down at the bowl. A pesto oil was drizzled on top of the tomato soup. But survivors didn't eat whatever their captors gave them, not even if it smelled delicious.

"You have the first bite," I said.

"Me?"

"What if it's poison?"

Rien let the spoon drop back in the bowl and tilted his head back to laugh. The warmth in his laugh sent a strange thrill through me. He seemed genuinely amused.

"Are you kidding me?" he said. "I could slice your throat open right now if I wanted to."

I stared down at the bowl, not saying anything. I wasn't sure what a survivor would say to that. Probably something witty. I was still sinking into the part, though. I only scowled.

"Fine. Have it your way."

With a smirk, he put the spoonful of tomato soup in his mouth. His Adam's apple bobbed as he swallowed, the underside of his chin dark with stubble. Why was I looking at him like that? He had taken me hostage. Survivors didn't fall for their captors, no matter how handsome.

"See? No poison."

"I'm not hungry," I said, looking away. My stomach growled again, betraying me.

"Your body is hungry."

"That's different."

"You're right." He set the spoon back into the bowl and put it down on the tray. "There is a big difference between you and your body. Your body, for example, might want the pleasure I have to offer you. Even if you don't want it yourself."

I didn't respond. I didn't know what he was going to do, but he only sat there next to me, breathing and watching me for a few moments. My fingers moved slightly at my side. I was definitely beginning to get my body back. Maybe I could fake being paralyzed until I had the chance to get at him. If I could jump up and choke him around the neck until he lost consciousness. Then I could run.

Who are you kidding, Sara? I thought. *You aren't a daring hero. What if it doesn't work? Then he'll kill you.*

No. I was a survivor. I could figure out how to get away. I just had to wait for the right opportunity.

"Tell me about yourself," he said finally, breaking me from my thoughts.

"Me?"

"I want to know more about how you came to be here."

"Sure," I said, breathing deeply. Just having him sit next to me was bringing back the memory of his fingers deep inside of me, and I was fighting to keep the thoughts at bay. I didn't want him to know how deeply he had affected me with his offer of *"pleasure."*

"Start at the beginning."

"I got a call from my agent. He said that Gary—Mr. Steadhill—wanted someone for a temporary role."

"No," Rien said. "I mean, the beginning."

He leaned over the couch, setting his elbow on the cushion back and resting his cheek against his knuckles. His body touched me, his hip grazing mine, and the heat that spun through my body made my thoughts slow and muddy.

"The beginning?"

"When you were a child. Tell me about your childhood. What led you to acting?"

I frowned, not knowing why he would care at all. The back of his hand idly skimmed along my arm. Immediately I felt myself opening up again to him, wanting his touch. Surely he knew what he was doing to me. But he thought that I was still paralyzed. I licked my lips and began.

"I never knew my dad. He left my mom before I was born. We were poor. I never really had anything. Then my mom got pregnant again with my sister, and we *really* didn't have anything."

"By a different man?"

I flushed. I never talked with anyone about this. I didn't speak about my family much, and in Hollywood nobody asked. Family was unimportant, meaningless, unless you had a connection to a higher-up in one of the studios. Acting families were the only families that mattered.

"Yes," I said.

"Did you ever know him?"

"No."

"You don't like to talk about him?"

"He wasn't part of our family."

"Who was he?"

"Nobody." My skin burned in shame.

"You're a terrible liar," Rien said. His fingers gently stroked my arm, going farther up and down with each pass.

"I'm not."

"Who was he?"

"He was a client," I spat.

Rien raised his eyebrows. I wanted to hit him then, punch him right in the face. I could see it in his eyes. He was judging us all, judging my mother for selling her body. Judging me.

"A client," he repeated tonelessly.

"I told you we were poor," I said.

"And then?"

I breathed out in relief and looked away from Rien. I would survive. I remembered surviving back then, when my mom went out late at night and slept with any guy who would pay her. Yes. I was a survivor. So was she. She had done whatever it took to survive.

"Then? Then I grew up taking care of my sister. We were on and off the streets. I hated it. When I turned eighteen, I left and came to Hollywood to try and make it."

"Have you made it?"

"Sure," I said, sarcasm biting into my words. "Of course I've made it. Look at me. I'm on a leather couch, giving an interview of my life story. If that's not making it, what is? I'm bigger than fucking Oprah Winfrey. I'll give you my autograph later, if I can ever move my paralyzed hands again."

A small smile crept over his face.

"So that's why you took this job."

"So that I wouldn't have to fuck a guy to make rent? Yeah, that's why I took the job. That's why I take every job."

"I'm sorry." He pressed his lips together. It was stupid, but he looked so sincere that I actually thought he was sorry. I felt sorry for myself, anyway. What a stupid story. What a stupid life. I should've stayed with my mom and sister. I should've helped them more. One measly check every now and then was ridiculous. I wasn't going to become an actress, and what's more, I didn't even want to act. I just wanted to get as far away from my real life as possible.

I bit my lip. I wasn't there anymore. I was here. I had to take care of myself here. And this was about as far away from real life as I could get.

"Here," he said. He picked up the bowl of soup. "You're hungry. Eat."

I opened my mouth, not knowing what had changed between us, only that something had. He held the spoon to my lips and warm soup spilled over my tongue. I swallowed, trying to think about anything besides the memories Rien had stirred. I didn't want to talk about my past. I didn't care about my past self. I was a new person here, or that's what I wanted to be. And if I hadn't been so stupid as to take this job…

I swallowed the soup spoonful by spoonful. Rien didn't talk at all. He held the food to my mouth and I ate.

It was strange. Not being able to do anything else, I relaxed. For the first time in a long time, I didn't have to worry about what to do next. I didn't have to worry about being fed. Stupid as it sounds, I didn't feel half as scared now as I had back when I was a kid. Not even with a killer sitting next to me with a bowl of tomato soup in his lap.

Soon the bowl was empty. He fed me crusts of garlic bread, pinching off bite-sized pieces. I chewed the buttery bread, savoring it. Even the fanciest dinner on Melrose hadn't tasted as good. I felt stronger. Better.

Comforted, in the weirdest way possible.

"You believe me, then?" I asked, once the last of the food was gone. "That I'm an actress? That I'm not this guy's wife or whatever?"

"Of course I believe you."

"Then… are you going to let me go?"

"No."

My heart sank in my chest. After I told him all that, just to have him shoot down any possibility of escape–

"Why not?"

"How can I trust you enough to let you leave? You've seen me with one of my victims. You know his name." He shook his head, as though thinking it over and coming to a conclusion. "I can't."

"What are you going to do, then? Keep me here forever?"

"Maybe. Yes. That's a possibility."

Panic gripped my chest. The thought of staying in this room as a prisoner made me feel like the walls of bookshelves were shrinking, closing in on me.

"Rien. Please. I'll do anything you tell me to do. I'll go straight home and I won't tell anyone about this ever."

He raised his eyebrows, smiling.

"Anything?"

I flushed. Of course, he would think of that. I hated it. Hated him. But I would survive regardless.

"No," I said quickly. "Not *anything*."

His eyes closed to slits. His pupils relaxed, going out of focus, as though deep in thought about something. I considered trying to attack him right then. He was distracted; I might be able to use the bowl as a weapon. Hit him with it and knock him unconscious. But before I could decide, he stood up from the couch. He bent over and took the tray, then set it on the bedside. Then he went behind the couch. I couldn't see him, but I heard the bookcase open up. Light streamed in from the operating room.

"Come here," he said.

"I can't," I said. "I'm paralyzed."

"Don't lie to me."

"I'm not lying."

Rien leaned over the back of the couch and reached down to my stomach. For a split second I thought that he would touch me down *there* again, and despite everything, my body responded by clenching inside, aching for it. Revulsion filled my mind, both at the memory of his touch and at my own body's betrayal.

But he did not touch me there.

Instead, his fingers moved to my waist, tickling me and knocking me off guard. I yelped; my legs jerked up involuntarily and my arms clutched my waist. His eyes met mine, and I saw a twinkle in his irises. *I got you,* the twinkle said. *You can't fool me. You're not a survivor yet.*

"You think I don't know when my own injections wear off?" he said, grinning. "Come on."

CHAPTER TWELVE

Rien

"You're a horrible liar," I said. I waited patiently by the bookcase as she stood up. "Is that why you've never made it as an actress?"

"I'm a method actor," she said. "I'm not supposed to lie."

She smoothed her dress down over her thighs. I wanted to throw her back down onto the couch, to plunge my fingers into her again and make her scream. It was so fun, this new kind of torture. But no, not now.

"What's method acting?" I asked, trying to tear my thoughts away from her creamy skin, her shaped calves.

"You've never heard of it? That's how Marilyn Monroe acted. It's all about becoming the character, instead of pretending to be the character."

"What's the difference?"

She opened her mouth to answer, her full pink lips pursing. Then she saw the open door and what was beyond it, and horror flashed across her face.

"I don't know if I want to go in there," she said. "What are you going to do?"

"You'll see," I said. "Don't worry. I won't hurt you."

"I don't want to see him."

Her voice was weak. I wanted to either comfort her or slap her across the face, I wasn't sure. She had lied, sure, but I didn't mind that so much. Not with how easy it was to pick out her lies. There was something that she was holding back, and I knew she was stronger than she appeared. So instead I waited, silently, until she stepped forward. Then I hit the switch on the side of the medical cabinet and the bookcase swung shut.

"What's the difference?" I asked again. She stared ahead at the operating room table in the middle of the room.

"Regular acting is all about pretending. You wear masks." Her voice was soft, the words coming out almost automatically.

"And the way you do it?"

"With method acting, you're not pretending. You're living. If your character is angry, you feel that anger." Her jaw clenched, and I could see something inside her rearrange itself into a definite hardness.

"Meisner called it *living truthfully under imaginary circumstances*," she said. She stood very still.

"Then let's pretend this is a stage," I said. I put one hand on her elbow and she twitched, then took a step forward. "It's a surgeon's stage, is what they call it. The operating room."

"You don't operate," she whispered. "You kill."

"It doesn't matter. We're both here now, living truthfully. Aren't we?"

Another flash in her eyes. Something bothering her.

"Come on, then," I said, cajoling. My hand cupped her elbow, and she let me lead her.

She shuffled over slowly, awkwardly. I could tell that the injection was still muting her movements. I had nothing to worry about with her. She'd be back to normal within the night, if a bit sore tomorrow. I led her through the operating room to the waiting room, and let her go to the bathroom while I waited by the open door. Then I took her arm and led her to the side of Mr. Steadhill. The silver nitrate had scabbed over his face properly, and when she saw him she blinked hard. She didn't turn away, though.

That was a good sign.

"Wait here," I said.

I went back over to my medical cabinets. I took out a scalpel and a black permanent marker from the first drawer. When I turned around, her eyes fixed onto the blade. She took a step back, and her eyes widened. I walked to the other side of the operating table. Mr. Steadhill began to moan behind the gag.

Pulling the cap off of the permanent marker, I motioned for her to come closer. She did. Her breathing was shallow.

"There are a lot of ways to kill someone," I said. I slid the drape down on Mr. Steadhill's chest. Thin tufts of dark hair spotted his skin. I drew a circle on the middle of his chest with the thick marker.

"This is the heart," I said. "The breastbone covers most of it, and even if you got past that, you'd have to slice through the pericardium. Too hard." I made an X over the heart.

"But this," I said, drawing a line on his neck, "is where you would have to cut if you wanted to slice the jugular. It's a quick death. Thirty seconds, on the high end. You bleed out quickly, very quickly. Like being guillotined. Much easier. Less satisfying, for some." I thought of Gav. "But easier to accomplish."

"Why are you telling me this?" she asked.

I stood up straight and turned the scalpel around. Holding it by the blade, I offered it to her.

"You wanted to get out of here," I said. "I'm showing you how."

Her lips parted when she realized what I was saying. The scalpel hung between us, the blade silver in the light of the operating room. Underneath, Mr. Steadhill squirmed, but I did not want her to pay attention to him. I wanted to be able to trust her, I really did. But there was only one way to do that.

"Kill him."

Sara

"Kill him?"

I stood in shock, staring down at the silver blade in Rien's hand.

"Yes," Rien said.

His word was soft, calming. I breathed in and reached out for the scalpel. He handed it to me, our fingers touching, and the touch sent a shiver through my body.

The scalpel looked so small now that I was holding it. The blade was delicate. It didn't seem like a weapon that could kill people. And yet... I looked down at Gary struggling to talk behind the cotton gag. His one good eye stared at me, straining to communicate as he made noises that sounded completely unintelligible.

"Why do you want me to kill him?" I didn't know what else to say.

"If you kill him, then I know I can trust you."

I looked up at Rien. His eyes burned golden under his dark hair. He was wild, and I saw something in his eyes that made me doubt the truth of what he said.

"Will you trust me? Really? Once I kill him?"

"It would make it easier. It would show me that you would never tell. You wouldn't have ever seen me kill. You would be the killer."

I looked down at Gary, who was screaming a muffled scream. He thought I would do it. His eye looked terrified up at me.

Would I do it? Could I be that character? Would a survivor do it? I looked down at where Rien had marked the skin on Gary's neck. One cut. One cut and I would be free.

Maybe.

Of course, there was no guarantee that Rien would keep his word. I swallowed and leaned forward, resting the scalpel against Gary's neck. My hand was trembling. I imagined pushing down, slicing through the skin—

My body was shaking, ready to spin away and run. This was a nightmare that I couldn't wake up from. Even my movements were dreamlike. I couldn't. Not now. I felt Rien's eyes on me and I realized what I was doing. I pulled the blade back.

"I can't do it," I said. "I can't kill him."

"Why not?" Rien said.

"Why not? I don't know. I…"

Because I can't.

Because a survivor would save herself without killing anybody.

Because I'm weak.

"He's a terrible person. He's killed hundreds."

Gary's voice struggled to be heard.

"He wants to talk," I said.

"You want to give him his last words?" Rien said. "Fine."

He hooked his finger into the gag and pulled it out. The tape holding it to Gary's skin ripped off one of his scabs. Blood began to flow down that side of his face again. Gary shouted at me, his voice hoarse.

"Kill him! Kill him!" He was frantic, spittle bubbling at the corners of his mouth. "Kill the motherfucking bastard now!"

I looked up at Rien, who only shrugged.

"Stab him with the knife!" Gary screamed.

"It's a scalpel," Rien said.

I looked down at the scalpel in my hand. It didn't seem big enough to kill anyone. I sure as hell wasn't about to attack Rien with it. It was a precision weapon, not something I could lash out with.

"Stab him! Stab him with the knife!"

"It's not a knife," Rien said patiently. "Knives are for butchers. What she's holding is a scalpel."

"Kill him!" Gary cried out. "For the love of God, kill him!"

"No."

I put the scalpel down on the table. My hands were shaking and I clasped them together in front of me. I wasn't going to take orders from anyone here. I wasn't going to become a killer. As soon as I let go of the scalpel, I felt a rush of relief. This wasn't right. It wasn't the right thing to do. Not for me, not for a survivor.

"I don't want to kill anyone," I said.

"He'll keep you locked up forever. He'll torture you. He'll—"

"Put the gag back in," I said to Rien. Rien raised his eyebrows, but stuffed the ball of cotton into Gary's mouth. Gary thrashed around angrily.

"I don't want to kill anyone. Not you," I said, looking down at Gary, then back to Rien. "And not you. Not even if it means staying here forever. Okay?"

"Okay," Rien said. His eyes had dimmed, the gold shimmer turning dull as he focused his attention elsewhere. "I won't kill him yet, Sara. In case you change your mind."

"Thank you," I whispered, stepping away from the operating room table. Behind me, Gary moaned. He was a victim. He wasn't a survivor. I didn't have to save him. I only had to save myself. I repeated that in my mind. I *would* save myself. I *would*. But I would have to be patient. Do things my own way. I was a survivor.

Rien opened the door back into the library and I stepped through. My hands were still shaking. Rien came in after me, carrying some things wrapped in what looked like a shirt.

I watched as the bookcase swung back after us, and a latch inside clicked shut. I still didn't see the way to open the bookcase. It must be a secret switch somewhere.

"Here's a shirt to sleep in," Rien said, tossing a white button-down shirt at me from the medical cabinet. "I have plenty of them for myself, but I'll have to see about getting you some other clothes. If you *are* staying here forever, that is."

He smiled a predator's smile. He thought he had me trapped. And maybe he did. I didn't see a way to get out. I couldn't kill Gary. I didn't know what to do.

"And here is some sterile fluid," he said. "For your contacts."

"My contacts?"

Right. I had forgotten about them. I took the fluid and stared at it dumbly.

"Oh, was that for the part? For acting like Mrs. Steadhill?"

"Yes," I said. God, was that earlier today? I had thought putting in the contact lenses would be the hardest part of the role. I hated touching my eyes. And now I was here, stuck in a library with a psychopath.

I glanced over at the bookcase. I hadn't seen how he opened it earlier. This could be my chance.

"Can I go back to the bathroom to take them out?" I asked. "I don't have a mirror here."

Rien stepped in front of me.

"Don't move," he said. Before I could step back, he had pinched my eyelid up with his thumb, holding the back of my head with his other hand so that I wouldn't move. I gasped as he plucked out one contact lens, then the other. I rubbed my eyes.

"There. Not that hard, once you're used to it." He looked from one of my eyes to the other. "So this is how you really look?"

I blinked. He didn't step away from me. His hand was still cupping the back of my head, his palm on my neck. The pure desire in his eyes made the muscles in my throat seize up. He wanted me and didn't care if I saw it.

"Green eyes. Beautiful."

Swallowing hard, I cast my eyes downwards. He looked at me like I was a victim. Like I was an easy mark. I didn't want him to see the survivor that I was trying to be. There was something in his gaze that tore away all of my pretenses.

"I'll see you in the morning," I said, not looking up at him. He went to the oak door, and I sat down on the couch, the shirt balled up in my lap. Even when he opened the door, it was dark behind him, and I couldn't see the other rooms.

"Good night," he said. "Sweet dreams." He closed the door behind him, and I heard a bolt slide shut. Then footsteps, leading away from the door. Then I was alone.

I wasn't staying here forever. But I wanted Rien to think that I'd given up. Soon, I would find a way to escape.

CHAPTER THIRTEEN

Rien

I tossed and turned in bed. Normally I slept in total comfort. You might think being a killer would make it hard to sleep at night, but really it was the exact opposite. Killing a guilty person soothed me. It was what I was good at. It was what I loved to do. In their suffering I found meaning.

Tonight, though, I couldn't rest.

Maybe it was the two other people in the house. Two people alive, breathing. Two people I was supposed to have killed. Bodies, I could handle. People? Not so much.

I rolled over to the side and picked up my phone to check the security cameras and alarm system. If the girl tried to escape, the alarm on the back entryway would go off as soon as she tried to open the door to the outside. And the door from the library to my half of the house was locked tightly. Still, maybe I should pick up another alarm, wire it all around the library…

What was I thinking? She was an innocent girl. She wasn't dangerous at all to me. She was only a toy.

My toy.

I thought of her lying down on the couch, and the image conjured up a flood of hormones. I touched myself idly, stroking myself through the sheets. What was it about her?

It was the layers, possibly. There was more to her under her skin than just a body. There was a mind that I had not yet come to understand. Villains were easy. Their motivations were simple: money, power, luxury.

But Sara... I didn't know what was inside that drove her to do anything. I had peeled off her fake eyes, dug deep into her body with my fingers but that still wasn't enough. Her soul wasn't visible to me, not yet.

The people on my operating table were always bare to me. They had a single, solitary purpose: to escape. They came to me because they were done with their previous lives. They wanted to escape. They wanted to disappear. And I made them disappear.

Just not in the way they wanted.

Sara was different. She had come into my house for a different reason. To pretend.

Looking over at the clock, I frowned. Midnight, and I still wasn't asleep.

Was she?

Just the thought of her made my cock jump to attention. I imagined her dark brown hair spread out over the couch. Her body, clothed only in my shirt, those full breasts straining against the buttons.

I thought of her breaths catching in her throat when I touched her. Was that pretending? There was more underneath, more than I could see.

Go to her.

Throwing back the sheets, I stood up and left the bedroom. I wanted to see what more there was to this girl. I wanted to tease it out, to find it for myself.

I wanted to take apart my toy and see what made it tick.

Sara

I'd spent an hour looking through the library. I ran

my fingers underneath the shelves of books along the walls, trying to find the hidden switch. I thought that it must be on the wall that led to the operating room. That was how he'd opened it before without my seeing. But I couldn't find anything.

Maybe it was one of the books. I skimmed my eyes over the shelves, trying to find something that would stand out. But of course it wouldn't stand out. It would be hidden. Secret.

I tried pulling out one book at a time at random, then handfuls, replacing them on the shelf when nothing happened. But there were thousands of books on the shelf. I couldn't check them all. Not tonight. The two injections he'd given me had messed with my system. My brain was fuzzy, even now. Or maybe that was just the exhaustion catching up to me.

It was almost midnight when I gave up on my search and turned off the light. Tomorrow I could search again. And the day after. I had time. As long as Rien continued to believe that I was resigned to my fate, I would have time to find a way to escape. He wouldn't kill the man, either, as long as he thought I might do it. If I was a survivor, I would have to pretend that I was unsure. I would have to pretend that I'd given up trying to escape.

But he saw through me!

That time. Yes. But not again. I would be the best actress I could.

I felt my way to the couch and lay down, drawing my knees up to my chest. In the dark, I couldn't see anything, not even a light from under the doorway. The library was sealed off from both sides of the house. The waiting room and operating room were on one side and Rien lived on the other side.

I wrapped my arms around myself as a chill went through me. On one side of me I had a killer, and on the other side a man who was going to die. Gary had lied to me, but I couldn't kill him.

Maybe you could, my mind said. *Stay unsure.*

Right. Maybe I could kill him. I tucked one arm under my head to use as a pillow. All I could smell was the leather of the couch and the dusty smell of old books. The shirt that Rien gave me was clean and sterile. When he'd touched me before, leaning over me, I had smelled his cologne. It was a delicate smell that hinted of peppermint and fresh air. I wanted to smell it again.

I shook my head in disgust. But then I realized that I could use this for my character. The survivor. She was pretending to want him.

Yes, I thought. I could do this. I could act as though he was attractive. I could pretend to be seduced by him. I could—

Footsteps came down the hallway. I held my breath. The bolt on the door snapped open.

I closed my eyes and pretended to be asleep. I had to calm down. My heart was pounding.

What did Meisner say about acting like this? *Transfer the point of concentration to some object outside of yourself - another person, a puzzle, a broken plate that you are gluing.*

Another object. The first thing that came to my mind was... a scalpel.

Fine. Yes. A scalpel. I was dreaming of a scalpel. My breathing slowed as I forced myself to concentrate. I saw the scalpel in my mind's eye. The silver blade. The small screw attaching the blade to the handle.

The door opened, creaking.

I fell deeper into thought. The scalpel shone in the light. I saw it turn in my hand, reflecting. I saw the blade, reflecting my face. And then, behind me, in the silver reflection—

"Sara."

The voice sounded far away, from behind a curtain. I

forced myself not to respond. In my mind, though, golden eyes stared at me from the mirror of the scalpel's blade. Golden eyes and dark hair.

"Sara."

Rien's voice was close, now, and I shifted my weight on the couch, stirring even as I told myself to keep my eyes on the scalpel, always on the scalpel. But the scalpel wasn't clean anymore in my mind. It was red. It dripped blood. My pulse grew fast again, my breaths became more shallow. And then—

"*Ah!*"

He touched me on the cheek, and I jerked awake as though I was really sleeping. My concentration was lost; I'd dropped the scalpel in my dreams.

My whole body cringed back, retreating into the leather couch. He grabbed my wrist. I twisted it away.

"Don't move," he said, grabbing my wrist again. My pulse began to thump in my ears. I wasn't concentrating on anything but the fingers wrapped tightly around my arm.

"What are you doing?"

"I won't hurt you. Don't move."

I struggled to pull away, and he stopped moving. As soon as I relaxed, though, he continued to pull me upright.

"You can fight if you want, Sara. But you won't be able to win. I'm much stronger than you." A whisper in the dark. A warning from the shadows. I bit my lip and let him move me like a doll.

He slid an arm underneath me and lifted up my body into a sitting position. I couldn't see anything; it was pitch black. All I could feel was his hand grasping my arm like a vise, the pressure of his upper arm keeping me up.

Then I felt the pressure of his chest against my back. He was bare-chested, and he shifted his weight forward so that I could feel him. His erection was hard against my lower back. A flash of terror went through me as a new thought found itself in my mind.

No. Not this.

A minute ago, I had told myself that I could do this. I could pretend to let him seduce me. If it would give me an advantage. Now that it was happening, though, I realized I had no other choice. I couldn't fight back; he would slice me open and think nothing of it. All I could do was distance myself. Act as though it was pretend. It was all pretend, wasn't it?

Then I thought of what he had done to me the first time and tears stung the backs of my eyes.

"Don't inject me with anything," I said, closing my eyes as though it would make the darkness go away. In my mind, the syringe was coming at me in the dark. I didn't know where it would come from. My heart pounded in my ears. *"Please.* No needles."

"No needles," he agreed. His voice was a soft whisper in my ear. For a moment, he sounded so gentle that I forgot to be afraid of him. I was scared, yes, scared of the darkness, but not of him. His hands softened on my arms, caressing my skin. "But don't fight me."

"I won't," I said. As terrified as I was, his words gave me a measure of relief. No needles. No paralysis.

If it got too bad, I could defend myself.

I didn't know what he was doing, but then he wrapped an arm around me, over my chest. His chin rested against my neck and he nuzzled my hair out of the way.

"Were you asleep?"

He talked to me like a lover. A crazed maniacal lover who was keeping me hostage in a library, but a lover nonetheless. His voice promised honeyed sweetness with its lilting words.

"Yes," I lied.

"Were you dreaming?"

"No."

Rien rocked me slightly back and forth, and in the total darkness my sleepiness began to catch up with me again. My heart slowed down, no longer pumping adrenaline through my body. He brushed my hair away and pressed his lips against my neck. A long, slow thrill seized my nerves.

"You were unconscious," he whispered. His breath skimmed the nape of my neck.

"Yes."

"It's like death, isn't it?"

"I don't know," I said. The image of the scalpel flashed again in my mind and I blinked it away. "I've never died."

"Descartes said it: *I think, therefore I am.* When you're not thinking, then, what are you? Isn't unconsciousness the same as death?"

"You're the anesthesiologist. You tell me. Or at least, that's what you pretended to be." He might've been lying to me about that, too.

"I am an anesthesiologist."

He was telling the truth. What was it about his voice that made me know he was telling me the truth? His thumb rubbed the side of my arm and I shivered.

"You're a murderer," I whispered.

"What's the difference? I put people under. Sometimes they come out of it. Sometimes not."

"You torture them."

"I tortured you." He hugged his arms around me a bit more tightly.

"Is that supposed to be comforting?"

"I don't deal in comfort. I deal in pain and pleasure. Specifically, other people's pain. My pleasure."

"But not for me."

"No," he said. There was something strange in his

voice when he said it, a kind of unease that I hadn't sensed in him before. Rien, who'd been utterly confident from the beginning, sounded unsure for the first time. It drew me even closer to him.

"What do you think?" he asked. The confidence in his voice came back as he changed the subject. "Do you lose your identity when you sleep?"

I leaned against him so that my head rested against his collarbone. His body was relaxed. I breathed in deeply.

"I'm not sure I'm awake now," I said. I let myself drift off, my heartbeat slowing. "This doesn't seem real. I might be dreaming. I might not exist right now at all."

"Are you a different person now than you were this morning, Sara?"

I opened my eyes. It was dark; nothing had changed. But I felt his muscles tense against my back.

"I'm nothing right now," I said. "I don't have an identity. I'm just a prisoner." *A survivor.*

His arms moved across my chest, pulling me against him. I gasped when he lay down onto the couch underneath me, pulling me back with him. His legs slid under mine, my feet grazing his ankles.

He was under me completely. I lay on top of him, my back against his chest. The back of my head rested on his shoulder.

His hands began to unbutton my shirt. One button at a time. I lay there, frozen, unable or unwilling to move. I'd just decided to pretend, hadn't I? But this didn't seem like pretending. His hands hypnotized me, caressed me. I breathed in deeply, feeling the pressure of my lungs as they swelled against his chest. Then his breath came back, resounding.

His cock was hard already. I could feel his erection pressing against the back of my thighs as I lay on top of him. Then he unbuttoned the top button of my shirt. His hands drew the fabric apart. The chill of the library air made my nipples hard. He cupped one breast with his hand, his thumb smoothing circles around the hard button.

Was this how it felt, when my mother slept with her clients? A sick dread twisted in my mind. He was a killer. He had me hostage. But at the same time, there was an unwilling pleasure that came from my body's reflexes. It mixed with the dread and fought it, and I didn't know what I wanted him to do. The hard length of his cock pulsed just under my thighs, and I felt myself clench involuntarily with desire.

How much of it did my mother hate? All of it?

I suppose she must have hated it. She was a stronger woman than I was.

Rien rolled my nipple idly with his thumb. The other hand moved down, his fingertips dragging across my skin. In the total darkness, my lips parted. I breathed in. The pads of his fingers were smooth. Long fingers. A surgeon's hands. I winced, thinking about his hand holding a scalpel, slicing open skin. He paused for a moment, and I let my breath out.

I could hear his breathing, too, right at my ear. He lay almost perfectly still underneath me, and I could feel the rise and fall of his chest as I rose and fell with him. Then he hooked the waist of my panties with his thumb.

I breathed in at the same time as he did. His chest swelled against my back, broad and warm. With his arms around me in a bear hug, he arched back against the couch, pulling down his underwear and my panties to our knees in one smooth motion.

I gasped as his bare cock twitched between my thighs, hot against my skin. To my embarrassment, I was already wet. I clenched my thighs together but he didn't even try to pull them apart. Instead his hands went back to my body. One hand kneaded the side of my hip just above my hipbone. The other hand moved back up, caressing my breast, moving across my stomach. I lay there and did not fight it, did not move.

Who was I now? Was I a survivor? How could I possibly be a survivor? I liked this. No, more than liked. I needed it. When he kissed the back of my neck, his tongue licking slow circles at the top of my spine, I moaned in pleasure. It had been long, too long, since a man had touched me so possessively.

He was hot underneath me and the air was chilly above. He drew down one side of the unbuttoned shirt and kissed me on the shoulder. I shivered.

"Do you like that?"

"Yes." The word was a whisper that could have been a scream. It was taking all of my energy not to touch myself. I ached for him, wanted him so badly.

He kissed me again, running a line of kisses along my shoulder and up my neck, then back.

"You fit perfectly in my arms, do you know that? Just the right size."

My lips parted when I felt his cock pulse again. It slid between my thighs, unbelievably thick. I whimpered as he adjusted his position under me. I was wet, oh god, so wet. It was easy for him to thrust upward between my thighs. His length ran along my folds but did not enter yet. I put my hand down between my legs and felt his tip poking out from between my thighs.

"Not yet," Rien murmured. He rocked back slowly, his whole length grazing me so lightly that it made me want to scream. How could he do this to me with his body? I was no survivor. I was nothing in his arms. I was only his.

Then he rocked forward, and again I felt his tip slide close to my entrance, wet with my juices. Then again. And again.

"Please," I said. My voice was hoarse with want. I

might have been faking at first, but there was nothing fake about the agony that trembled my body right now. My body was a hollow core that needed him to fill it. Tears rose to my eyes as he slid closer, then backed away again. *"Please."*

"Tell me what you want."

"I want…"

I couldn't say it. Damn me. I couldn't speak the words.

"Tell me."

"I can't…" I said, my voice catching in my throat. "I can't…" I reached down, touched his cock. He tilted his hips up, letting me guide him inside of me. As his tip went in, his hand brushed mine away. His fingers slid down over my clit. I breathed in sharply as he wet his fingers with my juices. Then he pressed down against my swollen clit and I cried out aloud.

In an instant, his other hand was around my neck and he thrust upward, piercing me with his cock. I screamed, and the hand around my throat tightened, cutting off my breath.

"Open your eyes," he whispered. I gasped, staring upwards into the darkness. Then he released the pressure, rocking back.

Before I could catch my breath, he did it again. The long fingers around my throat took away my air, and in the pitch black I saw stars flash before my eyes. I twisted against his grasp, but he had me pinned against his body with both arms. My hands clutched at his hand around my throat, but I could not tear him off.

"Ohhh," he groaned, thrusting upward into me, and the rumble of his voice made my body shiver deeply. I gasped as he released my throat, but he still held me tight. He rocked into me again, and I cried out in pleasure, my cry fading only when his hand came around my throat. But this time I was ready. I had taken a

breath. When he thrust up, I closed my eyes.

I could only breathe when he let me, and my gasps began to come in time with his rhythm. His thumb rolled over my tender clit, flicking it with every thrust. His swollen cock worked its way deeper and deeper into my core.

Rien was rough, but as his hands worked on my body, I felt a deeper pleasure begin to surface. This was a desire that I could never have admitted to myself. He was moving my body so that it would pleasure him perfectly. He was using me as a sex toy, his thrusts completely disregarding my cries. Nevertheless, I started to move along in his rhythm. As he thrust, I rocked my hips backward, meeting him as our bodies crashed.

My breaths came faster, even with his fingers held tight around my neck. He slid me up and down over his body, and his sweat and mine mixed with my juices so that every motion was slick. He rolled his hips upward and I felt the pressure inside of me rise and rise. With every roll of his hips, a gasp of pleasure escaped me. With every motion, he carried us both higher and higher. The rhythm of his thrusts grew faster, and now I could hear his heartbeat. It was pounding fast, and it matched my own.

I clenched around his swollen cock, needing it. Needing *him*. Using his arms as leverage, I rocked against him, riding his steel-hard cock.

Then his body tensed, his arms gripping me with a sudden pressure, and my orgasm ripped through me at the same time as his. The stars in the darkness turned into fireworks that splashed brightness across my vision. The pulsing ecstasy tore through me again and again, and I screamed aloud, riding him hard into another climax.

He shuddered upward and my body clenched, milking him, draining him completely. He breathed hard, his chest thudding against my skin with the pulse of his heartbeat. Inside me, his cock still throbbed in time with his heartbeat. If his body had been warm before, now it was so hot that I could barely stand to lean my head back against his shoulder.

We lay like that for a minute, our breathing calming down together.

Was this real? This was what I'd been looking for, every time I'd slept with a guy. This brutal possession of my body. The almost supernatural way he knew how I would react to his touch. The way he sent me reeling with wave after wave of orgasm. None of it was for show. We were in the dark. But he'd just given me the most pleasure I'd ever known.

This wasn't pretend. This wasn't what my mother had known. I was sure of it. His attention had been entirely on me the entire time, like he could read my mind.

I shifted, and he slid out of me. He helped me sit up, and a wash of dizziness passed over me. I lay back against the couch cushions. He stood up and pulled his underwear back up.

It was only when I heard the door opening that I spoke.

"What was that?" I asked. He paused, and even though the lights were off, I could see the expression on his face darkening.

"A character study," he said, finally. "I was having a hard time getting to sleep."

"Oh," I said, disappointment edging my voice. I don't know what kind of answer I was expecting. I don't know what kind of answer I wanted. I only know that at his words, a shiver ran through my body and it was all I could do to keep myself from going to him and throwing my arms around him. Stupid me. Stupid imagination.

"I hope you sleep better," I said. I tried to make my

words cold, but I couldn't. In the dark, he had taken me completely and then given me back to myself. I choked back the sentiment. He obviously didn't share it.

"I should be fine now," Rien said. "Thank you— thank you for not fighting too much. I hope you enjoyed it. Whether you were pretending or not."

CHAPTER FOURTEEN

Rien

I sat at the head of the operating room table. Gav was sitting at the other end with one of his own number eleven scalpels, making little cuts into the bottom of Mr. Steadhill's feet.

"I don't know what to do with her," I said, running a hand through my hair. Gav poked the blade between two of the toes, and Mr. Steadhill made a nice squealing noise. Gav always knew the right buttons to push.

"She in there?" He waved the scalpel at the secret door to the library.

"Yeah."

"Can I meet her?"

"No. You want her to see your face, too?"

Gav yawned, covering his mouth with his fist.

"No, I guess you're right. You can't just, you know?" He drew his finger across his neck.

"She's innocent. I can't kill an innocent person."

Especially not someone like her. I didn't know how to say that, though. There was something strange about her. Something I couldn't quite put my finger on. And other things, not so strange, that I could put my finger on. God, her body was delicious.

"Now you know how I feel," Gav said, watching my expression. "Careful, or you might fall in love with her."

"Ha! No, I'm keeping her locked up in the library. I only took her out this morning to let her go to the bathroom. I gave her a bagel. I don't know," I said, feeling like I was rambling. "It's a sticky spot to be in."

"Are you keeping her sedated?"

"No." I thought back to when I had paralyzed her, and a rush of blood ran down to my dick. I'd loved watching her eyes as I pleasured her. And last night…"I don't know. What would you do?"

"You know what I would do."

"No I don't."

"Hypothetically," Gav said, tracing the scalpel around Mr. Steadhill's big toe, "hypothetically I'm you. And I have this girl, an innocent girl, locked up in my library."

"Yes."

"And I'm falling for her."

"I'm not falling for her."

"And I'm *kind of* falling for her." Gav smiled. "Do I kill her, or do I let her go?"

"There's no other option?" I asked.

"She knows you're a killer."

"I haven't killed anybody yet," I said. "What if I let this guy loose?"

Mr. Steadhill looked up hopefully at me, growing silent for the first time in hours. Gav poked his foot again with the scalpel and he yelped.

"Of course not. Kill him. But you can't keep her here forever. You'll have to decide whether it's worth it to you to let her go."

"I can't let her go. If the feds see her leave my place, they'll just track her down and kill her themselves. Or send her to someone else like me, to make her disappear. She's got her foot in some messy business, here, Gav."

"You're telling me."

"You don't think I could just keep her here?" I asked, hating the pleading note in my voice.

"It's tough, keeping a girl locked up. I only lasted what, a week with my hostage? I couldn't handle it." He frowned. Blood began to stream down Mr. Steadhill's foot and onto the floor.

"Damn, I nicked a big blood vessel here."

I rolled my lab stool over to the medical cabinet and fished around in the drawer.

"I keep thinking that something will come to me. Some idea that will make everything okay." I pulled out a bottle of superglue and tossed it over to Gav. He caught it and opened it up.

"You wish. If you don't love her, kill her. Put her out of her misery."

I frowned. The girl was interesting. It was interesting to touch her. Interesting to talk with her. She'd surprised me with her boldness. I didn't want to swat her down. It didn't seem right.

"And if I do love her?"

"Do you?"

"God, no," I said. "But as a hypothetical."

"Rien."

"What?"

"You've never lied to me before." Gav grinned, applying superglue to the cut on Mr. Steadhill's foot. The blood stopped flowing.

"Who knows, maybe she'll decide that she can stand to kill this asshole. Then we're both murderers. Or rather, she's a murderer."

"That's a weak plan."

"It's all I've got."

"Pretty weak."

"You think so?" I scratched my chin. "Why?"

Gav raised his eyebrows at me.

"Seriously, Rien? Here, let me show you what'll happen." He mimed picking up a phone. "Hello, police? Hi, some crazy man kidnapped me and tortured me and forced me to kill a guy. Your high up guy at the CIA won't think twice about cutting you loose if that shit goes public. And like you said, if the feds get to her right away, she'll be dead in two seconds."

"Fine. I'll come up with another plan."

"Better hurry up before the feds realize this guy's wife isn't dead." Gav was back to cutting, this time around the pinky toe.

"I don't care about that. They have it all on camera. Two people come in here, no people come out. That's all I got paid for."

"You got paid to kill two people. A husband and a wife."

"So?"

"So the wife isn't the wife," Gav said, pointing the scalpel meaningfully at me. "And neither one of them is dead."

"And?"

"I'm just saying," he said, going back to the pinky toe, "you didn't really do the job you got paid for."

"You want my job? You think you can do my job?"

"No, I don't want your job! I'm just saying."

"God, Gavriel. Alright. Let me alone. I gotta think." I rubbed my hands over my eyes. This wasn't going at all the way I'd thought it would go. I wanted Gav to come up with an idea that didn't involve killing innocent people or getting caught.

"Alright," Gav said. He wiped up the mess under Mr. Steadhill's feet, spraying the tile with bleach before tossing the washrags down into the incinerator. He stopped at the door and looked back. "Want to come up for a barbecue this weekend?"

"Maybe. If I can figure this thing out."

"Hey, don't do anything drastic, okay?"

"Don't worry, I'm not some emotional pansy like you," I said, not knowing if that was entirely true after all. After last night. "See you around, Gav."

"See you."

He left, and I was alone with Mr. Steadhill. I twirled the scalpel in my hand. Gav being more coldhearted than me? I wasn't falling for this girl. If anything, I was making her fall for me.

"This isn't like me," I said aloud, more to myself than to the man tied down on the table next to me. "I swear it. It's just a bit of fun, that's all. I can kill her whenever I want to."

Sara

Rien let me brush my teeth in the waiting room bathroom that morning. I washed up as best as I could without a shower. I wanted to ask him if I could take a bath in the other side of his house, but when I came out, he was rubbing at the dark circles under his eyes. He locked me up in the library and then went back to the operating room, leaving me to eat a bagel alone. I heard voices through the bookshelves, and occasionally Gary's screams. I tried to ignore them.

After an hour, he came back into the library wearing a different shirt. I didn't know how to act around him. He moved as confidently as he had before, treating me like nothing had happened. I was nervous, panicky. I tried to act as nonchalantly as he did.

"Thank you for breakfast," I said, motioning with the bagel.

"Sure," he said. "Did you sleep well?"

"Yeah." I thought of what he'd said earlier. "Even the part where I lost my conscious identity."

"Really? I didn't think I was that good."

I choked on my bagel with nervous laughter. Rien offered me the glass of water. I took a drink and wiped my tears away, coughing. All of the uncertainty that I'd carried with me through the night burst out of me.

"Oh," I said, breathing deeply. "Okay. Alright."

"Did you want anything else to eat?"

"I'm fine. Rien," I said, catching him about to leave.

"Yes?"

"Why did you come in here last night?"

He raised his eyebrows slightly and leaned against the door.

"I wanted to know more about you."

"Like what my nipples feel like in the dark?"

"Sure." He smiled, and I felt a twist of unease work its way through me. Was that all it was?

Don't be silly, Sara. Of course that's all it was.

I looked at the bookshelves, my eyes unfocused.

"Did you want to talk?" Rien asked. He came back over to the end table and set the tray down. The plate clinked lightly against the silver.

"There's not much to say, is there?"

He looked at me without speaking for a moment. His gold eyes ran down my body, resting on the curve of my hip where his shirt stopped at my thigh.

"Why did I come to you last night?"

"You're asking me?" I said. "I don't know. Maybe it was your unconscious identity making the moves."

He studied me carefully. Under his hard gaze, I felt my skin burn. I turned back to the bookshelves, resting my fingers lightly against the spines of the books.

"You're different in the light," he said finally.

"Yeah, lots more photons bouncing everywhere."

"You're different. More sarcastic. Colder."

He stepped toward me, and I could feel his presence pressing the air back. The library felt different now. Hotter. Wetter.

"You just can't see me scowling in the dark," I said flatly.

"Is that what you call it?"

I flushed.

"I don't know how not to be sarcastic," I said. I pulled a book out of the bookshelves and flipped through it, not seeing the words.

"You weren't sarcastic last night."

"I don't know what last night was."

Rien leaned against the bookshelves and looked up into my face. I bit my lip and looked straight at him. He was never different, I thought. He was always cool, unflappable. He was the most confident person I'd ever met. I'd only ever seen under that calm confidence once. Last night.

"Why did you want to be an actress?" he asked.

"This again?"

"Is it the fame? Money?"

"Why are you asking me?"

"I want to know why you wear so many masks."

"Everybody is fake," I said, shoving the book back into the shelf. "Why shouldn't I be good at being fake?"

"That's not an answer."

"Sure it is."

"I want a real answer."

I couldn't tell him the truth to his face, not when he was looking at me like that. So I turned away and sat back down on the couch.

"I never wanted anything, okay? We were poor."

"That doesn't make sense. It sounds like you would want everything, then."

"Why?" I frowned.

"You said it yourself: you had nothing."

I shook my head. My chest tightened as I thought about it.

"You don't understand. That was why. I couldn't beg my mom for candy when we were all eating bread for dinner. I couldn't want anything. One time on my birthday, I asked my mom if I could have a Barbie. A

Barbie! That shit costs like twenty dollars new. And I saw the look on my mom's face when I asked. It was so much hurt in that look."

Rien was staring at me. I could tell. I could feel his gaze on me, like I felt his fingers all over me last night. It was a palpable stare, and I shifted in my seat.

"I didn't realize it until later. What it would have cost her to buy me a Barbie. What it cost her just to buy the bread we ate. And when I realized it, I stuffed all that want so far back inside of me that I never wanted anything at all."

Tears burned the backs of my eyes. Everything she had done for me and my sister! There was no way I could possibly repay her for all she had done for us.

"You did want things, though. You just didn't tell her."

"No!" I looked up. "That's what I'm saying. I stopped wanting anything. Inside. I convinced myself that I didn't want happy meals, or toys, or even a soda from the 7-11. I convinced her that my favorite lunch was mayo on toast, because that's all we could afford. I saw the look on her face when my sister whined about what we ate.

But it wasn't just her. I convinced myself. I buried every single want I ever had deep down, burned away all the desire. I covered it with concrete and cinder blocks and locked it away for good."

A sob rose in my throat and I cut it off, biting down on my tongue. I didn't want to cry in front of him. Not him. Not now. What happened to keeping myself locked behind a mask? I was failing, miserably. He had torn down all of my screens and now I was sitting in front of him as exposed as if I was naked.

Rien came over and sat on the couch. He put his hand on my knee. I wanted to shake him off. I wanted to pull him into an embrace. I wanted to kill him.

"You'd make a good serial killer if you decided to change careers."

It was such a strange comment that I burst out with one short laugh. Rien pulled out a handkerchief from his pocket and handed it to me.

"Oh, yeah?" I asked. "Why?

"Concrete and cinder blocks? That's basically how you get rid of a body."

I bit my lip. He smiled at me and kissed the top of my head. I couldn't help it; I leaned into his arm and savored the pressure of his lips. His warmth.

"So that's why you want to be an actress."

I nodded, wiping the tears from the corner of my eyes.

"Yes. Because every character has a motivation. Every character comes with a set of goals, desires, dreams. It's wonderful to slip into a part and not have to think about anything except that one motivation that keeps you going. Pretending to want something is almost as good as wanting it."

"You don't have any motivations at all?"

"No. Never." I twisted the handkerchief in my lap.

"I don't believe that. It's a mask, that's all."

His face flinched when he saw my expression.

"You think this is a mask I'm wearing on top of my real self?" I asked. I balled the handkerchief up, blotting the tears angrily from my cheeks. "It's not. It's all there is. It's a bunch of masks, one on top of the other. There's nothing underneath."

"That's not true."

"I'm not lying."

"I didn't say you were lying. But it's not true. There's more to you than just that. You have passion in you. Dreams. It's not empty inside. Trust me. I've met a lot of empty people."

Suddenly, I was sad. I was pretending. Always

pretending. Even now. Pretending to pretend. Was that really all my life was?

"Thanks for believing in me," I said listlessly. "The one person to tell me to follow my dreams is a psycho serial killer."

"Psycho? Excuse me?"

"You rip people's faces off."

"Rip is such a rough word. I cut their faces off. Surgery is a precision skill."

"Whatever." I blew my nose.

"You know, you remind me of a quote. 'If I had a desire, it would be to be free from desire.'"

"Sounds like me. Who said that, the Dalai Lama?"

Rien smiled.

"Charles Manson."

"No way."

"Sounds like you, huh?"

"Okay. Okay. I walked right into that one." I chuckled sadly.

Rien stood up, and I wanted to take his hand and pull him back down onto the couch. Oh, God! I wanted a serial killer to comfort me. I felt so goddamn empty.

"I've got to go to the grocery store, my dear little psycho," he said. "I'll be back." He reached over to the shelf and pulled out a book. It landed on the couch cushion next to me.

"Manson: A Biography," I read aloud.

"Maybe he'll give you some good ideas," Rien said, his eyes twinkling golden brown. "For what you want."

"From the grocery store? I want a cupcake."

"Sara, I mean it." His expression softened. "Think on whatever it is you want. Or if you really do want... nothing. I'd like to know."

"What do you want to know?"

"What you want. What makes you tick. What makes you you. Surely you're not such a psychopath as

Manson. Or maybe…"

"Maybe what?"

"Maybe he was the sane one."

"Only you would think that," I said. I held up the book in front of my eyes so that Rien could not see me cry. I did not want him to know how much it meant to me that someone cared about what I wanted, even a little. The words blurred behind my tears as the door closed behind him.

CHAPTER FIFTEEN

Rien

How could I kill her? I'd only just begun to understand her. I walked down the sidewalk meditating on the strange fascination that had come over me.

She was my plaything, yes, but as I peeled back her defenses, I saw more to her than she saw in herself. I could not cut out that consciousness, no, not with what I saw there. I could understand her frustration, at least in part. There was no way I could tell her, though.

My life on the surface might have been the opposite of hers. My family was rich, ambassadors who traveled from one European country to another. On the surface, I'd gotten everything I wanted. My mother and father had kept me carefully clothed. They bought me cars, food. They gave me money and arranged dates with other embassy children. But there had been no love. Everything I began to love, they took away.

I only ever loved one girl, and they took her away, too.

I shook the thoughts from my head. The Los Angeles sun beat down on my head, and the whole world looked too bright to be real. Along the street, I passed by shops and bars full of fake people chattering about fake nonsense. All I wanted was to get back to her.

In the grocery store, I ran my hands along the aisles, picking out things I thought she might like. A ribeye that would pair nicely with the Cabernet vintage I'd been saving. Heirloom carrots to add to the mashed potatoes.

Once I reached the end of the aisle, I realized I was whistling.

This girl, what was she doing to me?

I bought my groceries, exchanging polite smiles with the cashier. I would have to be more careful, I thought. Today I had the excuse of a date. If this turned into a longer arrangement, though, I would have to spread out my shopping. Buying food for two would be an easy way to get caught.

Turning the corner back onto the street, I thought of the cupcake store I'd be passing by. My mind was on flavors. Chocolate? Strawberry? I wasn't looking out. I wasn't thinking.

I'd forgotten that not thinking gets me in trouble. Stupid. Careless.

I didn't see him waiting for me in the alley.

Sara

I picked up the Manson book that Rien had left for me on the couch. I turned through the pages, skimming it. The first part was all about his childhood, so I flipped through to the middle. There was a statement in his trial testimony that caught my eye. I leaned back on the couch and read through the page.

"We're all our own prisons, we are each all our own wardens and we do our own time. I can't judge anyone else. What other people do is not really my affair unless they approach me with it. Prison's in your mind. Can't you see I'm free?"

Right. Free as a goddamn bird. I looked around at the library walls and laughed. I remember back in kindergarten, my teacher had told us all that if we could read, we could always go and explore new places in our minds. We would never be constrained.

My kindergarten teacher had never been locked in a library by a serial killer, though.

Rien

Vale stepped out behind me, the muzzle of a gun prodding my lower back from under his jacket.

"Rien," he growled.

"Nice to see you too, Vale," I said. Such carelessness. And yet, all I could think in that moment was: *If I died, how would she escape?*

Vale shoved me into the alleyway in front of him and I raised my free hand up casually. "What's up?"

"Why don't you tell me?"

"I don't know what you're talking about."

"First, against the wall."

I turned and waited as he patted me down. In my mind, I ran through my story. I would have to play dumb. I'd killed the couple, sure, I'd killed them. Well, they were locked in my house, anyway, and my security system was unbreakable. It came out to the same thing. Even if I wasn't planning on killing Sara. Vale kicked my leg out and patted my thighs.

"Feeling frisky? Vale, all you have to do is let me take you out to the club sometime. You've got a real Paul Newman thing going on with the blond hair, blue eyes. Maybe we could get you in the pictures."

"How about you let me buy you a drink," Vale said, grabbing my arm once he was satisfied I wasn't carrying a weapon.

A drink? I didn't want to talk to my boss now.

"It's a little early."

"You might need one. I know I do."

He led me back down to the street and into a shitty dive pub. We went back into a corner booth and he snapped his fingers for the waitress.

"This is a real classy place, Vale," I said, running a napkin along the sticky tabletop. "I bet if we ask them, they'll even wipe the table down for us."

"Two whiskeys. Neat," Vale called to the waitress, who had taken a break from studiously ignoring us.

"Make mine a double. On the rocks. Can you put my groceries in the fridge behind the bar there?" I asked, flashing a winning smile. "Thanks."

The waitress came back with two whiskeys and set our drinks in front of us. Vale threw down a crumpled ten dollar bill.

"You're flying high, aren't you? What do they pay spooks nowadays?"

"Not enough for dealing with shitheads like you."

Vale leered at me and threw back his whiskey. I sipped mine. The waitress sat in the front of the bar, out of earshot. Vale dropped his voice anyway.

"I hear rumors flying around. Rumors that Susan Steadhill was killed."

"Yeah?" I said. "You're welcome."

"Rumor is that you didn't do it."

I licked my lips, uncertain of how much to tell him. If anything.

"They came into my house. I killed them."

"Yeah, that's what the surveillance tapes show."

"And?" I raised my eyebrows, pretending to be sincere. I thought about what Sara had told me about method acting. I had killed them, I told myself. They were dead. If I believed it, he would believe it.

"And I'm not buying it," Vale said, eyeing me warily. "Because I got this rumor tells me that Susan was killed before she ever got to your house."

"You have proof of that?"

"No. This rumor didn't come with a body."

"That's a shame."

Vale slammed his glass down on the table.

"Where's Susan Steadhill?"

I took another sip of my whiskey. I'd always been good at lying. Kids who hate their parents are always good at lying.

"I don't know. I thought she was dead. I thought I killed her."

"Don't joke about this."

"You're the one who sends me the witnesses. I just get rid of them once they walk in. The woman who came in said that she was Susan Steadhill."

"Yeah, well, she might not have been."

"Not my fault." I went to slide out of the booth. If that was all he had, he had no business keeping me here.

He grabbed me by the arm. I winced.

"We might have killed an innocent person, Rien."

"When did the U.S. government start caring about that? Hold on. Strike that. When did *you* start caring about that?"

"We don't know where the wife is. I don't have a body."

"So she could still be alive?"

"Maybe," Vale said.

"Have you tried looking in Brazil?"

"Ha. Real funny, Rien."

"I haven't seen her. Can I go now?"

"Sure, sure. You have their teeth for me?"

Shit. There it was.

"No."

"No?"

"I was out on a grocery run, for Chrissake."

"I need proof, Rien. I need to find out who that girl is and do cleanup."

"Yeah." *I need to find out who she is, too.*

"And I need proof that it was Steadhill who came in alongside the girl. They might have both hired body doubles for all I know."

"Okay."

I took the glass of whiskey and shot the remainder. I didn't know how to deal with Vale. He rarely asked for proof, but when he did, he meant it.

"So?"

"So what?"

"So give me the teeth. Let's go back right now."

"I don't have them out yet."

"Why not?"

"I'm having some fun with their bodies." That at least was true. "I haven't incinerated them."

Vale's eyes narrowed.

"You're a sick fuck, Rien."

"Yeah, well, good luck getting someone who's not a sick fuck to do your dirty work for you." I stood up from the table.

"I want their teeth. I'll stop by tomorrow."

"No can do. I'm busy all day."

"Tomorrow night."

I pretended to consider.

"I'm not asking, Rien. I'm in a mess of confusion and I need to know who's dead and who's not."

"Fine. Tomorrow night. Now, if you'll excuse me, I have to buy a cupcake."

Sara

I continued reading the book. I had to say, Manson wasn't all insane. I mean, he was mostly insane, but all of his thinking made sense, in a weirdly consistent sort of way.

Pain's not bad, it's good. It teaches you things. I understand that.

Creepy. I understood why Rien had this in his library.

Living is what scares me. Dying is easy.

And killing is even easier, apparently. I flipped forward again to a random page.

Anything you see in me is in you. If you want to see a vicious killer, that's who you'll see, do you understand that? If you see me as your brother, that's what I'll be. It all depends on how much love you have. I am you, and when you can admit that, you will be free. I am just a mirror.

I paused there. Was that how Rien saw himself? When he killed people, was he doing it out of hate, or out of something else? From what I'd read so far, Manson didn't think that killing was bad, because dying wasn't bad. Which made sense, in a crazy-ass serial killer way. There wasn't any right or wrong in his world.

Then I hit one of the last pages. He was talking about Hollywood. I pulled the book closer.

I lived in Hollywood and I had all that, the Rolls Royce and the Ferrari and the pad in Beverly Hills. I had the surf board and the Beach Boys and the bishkis and the Neil Diamond and the ramskam and the Jimmy shriffen and the Elvis Presley's best of bestlies and all them guys. The Dean and Martins and the Nancy Sinatras and the goffs and sofrins, "Will you do it to me? I hear you do it good honey" and all that kind of "Will you come up to my house later?" So I went through all that and I seen that was a bigger prison than the one I just got out of and I really didn't care to go back in prison. See, prison doesn't begin and end at the gate. Prison is in the mind. It's locked in one world that's dead and dying, or it's open to a world that's free and alive.

My mouth dropped open. I don't know how many

times Rien had read this book, or if he even knew what was in it, but the words struck me with the force of a slap on the face. Was that what he thought I wanted as an actress? I didn't want that. I didn't care about fame and fortune or any of those things.

No, that was what Rien had already. The sexy car, the luxurious penthouse. He had the Hollywood dream, and all it took to get there was killing people. He took fake people living fake lives and killed them. Because, after all, death wasn't bad. Living a lie was the worst sin of all.

So Manson said. And he repeated his words. *Prison was in the mind.* And Hollywood was a bigger prison than any jailhouse. I thought I understood. Or at least, I began to understand. I don't know if I really could ever understand Rien.

He'd told me to think about what I wanted.

What did I want?

I couldn't read this anymore. I set the book down on the couch and stood up. I stretched. I rolled my neck.

And I had nothing else to do.

"Prison is in the mind, Sara," I said out loud. "I can go anywhere." Just like in the Reading Rainbow song. I hummed it as I looked through the bookshelves. There must be something that could take my mind off of serial killers.

There were a ton of medical books on the shelves. *Clinical Anesthesia. A Manual of Surgical Procedures. Respiratory Physiology: The Essentials.* Even the titles made my head spin. I turned to look at what else he had. Old histories. Books in French and Greek. I sighed as I ran my fingers down the shelf.

"Not too much of a fiction guy, huh?" I murmured. But then, it made sense. Rien seemed to hate anything fake. He didn't want to live in a pretend world.

Good for him. It would make my days a lot more

boring, though, if I didn't have anything to read.

The rest of his library was similar, but as I moved onto the back bookshelf that led to the operating room, things got a little better. There were some books on ancient children's fables that looked promising. And then a bunch of philosophy. I didn't really care for the heavy stuff, and my fingers brushed past Locke and Kant and Hume. But then I saw a title that looked familiar.

Man's Search for Meaning.

My mom had gotten a copy of that book from the library. I remember because I was thirteen, and we had just gotten evicted from our new place. The women's shelter we stayed at was across from the public library, and she'd brought it home to read. She'd fallen asleep and I remember picking the book up off of the floor.

It was about the Holocaust, and how this guy had survived through years in a concentration camp. I didn't understand it all when I was thirteen, but I understood why she had gotten it. It talked about how no matter how bad things got, you could still find meaning in life.

Well, things had gotten pretty bad for me, stuck in the library of a killer.

I reached out for the book, and as I slid it out from the shelf I heard a click. I jumped back as the wall began to move.

The bookcase spun open.

CHAPTER SIXTEEN

Rien

I picked up the cupcake for Sara–I decided on red velvet, with cream cheese frosting–and called up the forensics lab as I walked back home. I asked for Jake.

"Rien? You know you're not supposed to call me at this number," Jake hissed into the phone.

"Hey, Jake, good to talk to you too."

"Seriously, Rien—"

"Remember that time you almost got caught by your girlfriend with a body in your trunk and I drove it down to the dock for you?" I nodded to a woman walking her poodle as she passed by me.

"Rien, don't—"

"I'm calling in the favor, Jake."

There was silence on the other end of the phone. I could hear Jake shutting a door, and then his voice came back on the phone.

"Hell of a time to call, Rien. I'm in the middle of a big investigation. The whole lab is swarming with police right now, and not just the L.A.P.D. asshats. What do you want?"

"Can you run a search for me?"

"That's it? That's why you called me here?"

"It's important. I need you to run a search on Susan Steadhill. Mask it. I don't want anyone knowing you pulled the file."

"Susan Steadhill?"

"There's feds involved. I need to find her before

they do."

"I know there's feds involved."

"What? How do you know that?"

"What do you think the investigation is for? She's a federal witness and they lost her. It's all supposed to be very hush-hush."

"I pinky promise not to tell anyone," I said. "But if you hear about a lead, let me know. And pull that file."

"What do you want to know?"

"Anything. Everything. And while you're at it, anything you have on Sara Everett." Saying her name into the phone felt wrong. I don't know why. I shouldn't trust anyone, not in my line of work. But it felt bad to mistrust her, for some reason. Jake was talking, but I hadn't heard a thing he said.

"Sorry, what?" I asked.

"That's one of the girls."

"What?"

I stopped cold on the sidewalk. Two joggers scowled at me as they swerved around me onto the grass. How did Jake know about Sara?

"That's one of the girls who went missing this past week. Your boss was the one who contacted me, that Vale guy. Creepy dude, even for a fed. He had me run them all."

"What do you mean, run them all?"

"All females eighteen to thirty-five. Thirty-two missing persons matching that description across America. Three of them were the L.A. area, though. She was one of them."

I licked my lip. My mouth was dry.

"Listen to me. Don't tell Vale anything. Don't tell him that I was here. If you can, find a way to drop Sara Everett from his roster."

"Hey, I'm not getting involved."

"Jake—"

"Uh uh. No. I am not getting anywhere close to between the two of you. That's way over my pay grade, man."

"You owe me."

"A favor, yeah, but not that big a favor. I cross Vale, that crazy son of a bitch will have my head."

I breathed out shakily.

"Fine. But you'll let me know if you have any leads on Susan?" I needed to find the wife, and find her before tomorrow night. If I found the wife, then there would be options. Right now I had zero options. And if I was forced to kill Sara because of it—

I closed my eyes. The sun was so hot today. A perfect California afternoon. I couldn't give up my life here for her. Hopefully, I wouldn't have to.

"Sure. The feds are all over this one already, Rien."

"I know. Call me once you have the information."

One day. That's all I had, and then I would have to make a hard decision. I still didn't know what I would decide, if it came to that.

So I just had to make sure it didn't come to that.

Sara

I looked back over my shoulder at the oak door. Rien had left a while ago. I didn't know when he would be back. Still, this was my chance!

I went into the operating room. Gary was lying still on the table. At first I thought he was dead, but then I saw his chest rise slowly.

Just asleep.

I tiptoed across to the waiting room door and tried it. To my surprise, it opened up easily. I stepped into the waiting room. The lights were off, all except for a single small spotlight on that glass bowl that stood in front of the entryway. The little plastic shapes inside looked even more like they were trying to crawl out.

Trying to escape.

Quickly, as quietly as I could, I walked to the door to the outside. This was where I'd originally come in. If I could get out the door, I would be free. Free! I put my hand on the door handle and tried to turn it.

Stuck. I tried again, wiggling the handle, but it wouldn't even move. The door was bolted shut. The metal lock didn't have a turnkey or anything that I could see. It was a blank steel plate on the door. I tugged harder at the door.

So close! I was a couple of inches away from the outside world. I had to get out! I had to!

I looked around frantically. In my mind, I imagined Rien coming in through the front of the house. I imagined him finding the library door open. I had to get out somehow, but how?

The chairs in the waiting room were leather, but there was a metal stool next to the coatrack. I picked it up and swung it at the door handle. It crashed, bouncing off of the handle. Nothing. I swung again, harder this time, but it only bounced back again. I took a deep breath and swung with all of my power, aiming at the end of the handle.

This time the metal stool hit the handle so hard that the reverberation made me lose my grip. The stool flew back and crashed into the stand for the sculpture. I watched as the stand swayed, then tipped over completely. The glass bowl fell and shattered on the ground, sending glass and plastic pieces across the floor.

I stared agape at the broken bowl. From the other room, I could hear Gary screaming through the gag. I tried the door handle, but it was as stuck as before. I couldn't get out that way.

Shit. *Shit, shit shit.*

I brushed the glass pieces aside with my foot. What could I do? Where could I go?

There weren't any windows around. I didn't know what to do. In a daze, I picked up the stool and walked back into the operating room. Maybe I could break the huge glass window.

I swung the stool against the window. The stool bounced off so hard that my hand turned numb from the shock of the reverberation. I looked up. It didn't make so much as a dent. I dropped the stool, my energy spent. I couldn't get out of here. There was no way.

Gary was screaming at me from behind the gag. His one eye was completely white and glazed over, and that side of his face was one huge scab. His other eye stared wildly at me. I swallowed as I went over to him. I couldn't let him go if we had no way to escape. But I didn't know how to escape. Maybe he would have an idea.

Carefully, I pulled the cotton gag from his mouth. Blood and mucus spilled from the corner of his mouth. He coughed wildly, unable to talk.

Water. He needed water. I ran over to the sink and filled a plastic sample cup from the faucet. I put it to his lips and he drank, coughing.

"Straps," he said finally. His voice was scratchy. "Take off the straps."

"I can't," I said, shaking my head. "I—"

"You stupid little bitch!" he yelled. Spittle burst from his lips. "Take off these fucking straps!"

"I can't yet," I said, trying to explain my reasoning. "There's no way—"

"You don't trust me?!"

I stopped and stared at him. I hadn't even thought about not trusting him until he mentioned it. What was there not to trust? We were both prisoners in here.

"Is it because of what he said? Don't believe him! You can't believe him!"

Gary's voice was ragged in the air. I let him drink another sip of water. My mind was churning.

"I can't untie you. If Rien finds you untied—"

"I didn't kill them." Gary shook his head back and forth wildly. "I didn't. I swear it! It was a faulty valve in one of our factories."

I frowned.

"But you were convicted, weren't you? Isn't that why you're leaving the country?"

"You can't listen to what that maniac says. The feds are on our side."

I paused. He had said that the police had brought us here. But that didn't make sense.

"If that's true," I said carefully, "why haven't they come to rescue us yet?"

Gary shook his head, cracking the scabs on the side of his face. Blood began to run down his cheek.

"I don't know. Listen. *Listen*. He was in here with his friend earlier. He was talking about you."

I peered at him. I'd heard voices through the bookcase, but didn't know that someone else had been in there.

"Who was in here?"

"Some other guy. They're both killers. He was planning on killing you."

A chill ran through my neck.

"What? When?"

"He didn't say. He said that he was just using you for fun, and that when he was tired of you, he would kill you."

I blinked. *Kill me?* Rien said that? The chill in my body turned to an icy dread. Despite all that I had seen, I couldn't believe that he would kill me. Not for that reason, anyway. And yet...No. In my mind, I saw Rien's hand around my throat, squeezing.

I shook my head and refocused on the current situation.

"We need to figure out a way to escape."

"Let me go."

"Once we figure out a way to escape, I can," I said, trying to be patient. "But I can't yet."

"We can attack him when he comes in. Both of us against him. With knives."

"I can't. He'll kill us." He could have a gun kept away in the other side of the house. And even if he didn't, I'd felt Rien's power. He was *strong*. I didn't think I had a shot at him. And Gary looked like he was half-dead. There was no way we could take him.

And, God save me, I didn't want to kill him.

"He's going to kill us anyway."

"No. Listen to me—"

"This is our only chance! At least let me out so I can help us escape! Please, oh God, please, he's been torturing me for over a day!"

Gary's whine made me reconsider. I gulped. Maybe he was right.

"Okay," I said, reaching out for the strap. "But if he comes back—"

My fingers just touched the strap when I heard Rien's footsteps. I pulled my hand back.

Oh God. Oh dear God.

"No! Let me go! You stupid bitch, just let me go!"

I backed up toward the bookshelf. I couldn't cover this up at all. The glass globe was broken. Gary's gag was off, and I wasn't about to stuff it back in. I stepped back into the library. Gary's screams echoed across the operating room. I pushed the bookshelf, trying to close it but it wouldn't budge.

"I got your cupcake," Rien said, swinging the oak door open. "Lunch is—"

He stopped mid-stride and stared at me standing next to the open bookcase. His smile faded from his face.

Gary screamed from the operating room, his voice booming.

"You stupid bitch! You stupid bitch! You're dead now, you see? You're dead! We're both dead!"

Rien stared at me. His eyes were unreadable, calm as a lake sheeted over with ice. I couldn't have killed him, not while he was still looking at me. Even though I knew that he could kill me without a second thought.

He had done this. He had tortured that man. I shuddered, more at myself than at Rien. Even now, hearing the screams of his victim, I couldn't believe that he would harm me. There he stood, silent. The air was heavy with meaning.

"You're dead!" Gary called. "You hear me? Dead!"

Rien took one step toward me, and, like the prey cornered by the predator, I froze. Like a rabbit under an owl's gaze, waiting to be eaten. The tortured voice rose, spiraling outward through the rooms.

"Dead! Dead! Dead!"

CHAPTER SEVENTEEN

Rien

I slowly set the cupcake down, knowing I might have to kill her.

Check for weapons. Don't let them trick you.

So she'd gotten out of the library. I eyed Sara cautiously as I walked toward the bookcase. She didn't have a scalpel in her hands; in fact, she didn't seem armed at all. She wasn't going to fight. That was good. And from the look of it, Mr. Steadhill was still securely fastened to the table. From his screams, she hadn't let him escape.

"I—I pulled out this book," she stammered. "I didn't know what would happen."

Her eyes were bright with fear as I moved towards her. What surprised me was my reaction to her fear: I felt bad. I wanted to comfort her. I wanted to put my arms around her and tell her that it was alright, that she had nothing to worry about.

Where did this sudden concern come from? She was a toy, a hostage. She was nothing to me. But her fear made me feel... awful.

I nodded through the doorway into the operating room where Mr. Steadhill was thrashing his head from side to side and screaming a bloody storm.

"You went in there?"

"Yes." Her voice trembled. I longed to steady it, but I held back.

"Did you try to escape?"

She nodded, frozen in fear. Her hands clutched the bookcase as I came close. Her fingers were white. Poor girl.

"Well, at least you're honest," I said calmly. She must not even have broken the lock if my alarms hadn't gone off. "Did you take anything?"

"No. I tried to get out through the waiting room."

"Alright." I stood next to her, arms calmly at my side. No sudden movements. She was such a scared creature.

"I broke... I broke..."

"What is it?" She couldn't have broken the window; it was double paned and bulletproof.

"The globe."

My mind went dark. She didn't mean...

I walked into the operating room. Mr. Steadhill let out a torrent of shouting when he saw me.

"Killer! Fuck! Stupid bitch! You see what you did! You could have saved me! You fucking idiot piece of shit! Now he's going to kill us all!"

I stopped at the medical cabinet, taking out a syringe from the drawer. Without saying a word, I went to Mr. Steadhill and injected him with the sedative. His screams died down instantly.

Now the room was quiet, so quiet that I swear I could hear Sara's heart beating in fright. She followed me as I walked slowly to the waiting room.

The light I'd installed to spotlight my sculpture was shining on nothing. The globe had fallen to the floor. It had shattered. The plasticized claustrums were scattered across the floor. Some of them looked to be broken.

Gone. All my work of the past few years. In pieces.

I fell to my knees and began to pick up the shards. My little trophies. I could save them, I was sure of it. It would take some time. But I could do it. I had destroyed so much to create this one piece of art. It seemed impossible that it too should be destroyed. I brushed the pieces into my hands, collected them in my cupped palms. Yes. Only a few were broken. I could fix them. I would.

A piece of glass cut my finger as I reached for one of the claustrums. I only realized it when I saw the blood dripping onto the pieces I'd already collected.

"No," I whispered. I used my shirt to try to wipe off the blood, but it only smeared the red deeper in.

"No, no, no," I said. I tried to put down all that I had gathered up, but my hands shook too badly. Another piece fell and broke in two. I jolted back on my knees.

"I'm sorry," Sara said. I turned to see her in the doorway. I had not seen her come there. Careless. I was so careless. Her green eyes shimmered in the dim light. I shook my head as I reached to pick up the broken claustrum.

"I'm sorry," she said again, and then she was kneeling, her arms around me. "Don't cry. I didn't know—I was only trying to break the door handle. Please don't cry."

Don't cry? Was I crying? I touched my cheek and felt wetness. I stared at Sara in mute disbelief. Silhouetted from the light behind, she was a dark shadow in the doorway. And the tears blurred the world, made her hazy like a Hollywood star in the 1950s.

"I'm so sorry," she said. "I didn't know it was yours. I'll help fix it. Look, go put a bandage on your cut. We'll fix it together."

"Go back to the library," I said.

"But—"

"*GO!*"

I shouldn't have screamed. I never scream. Anger, sadness—these are not emotions that cross my heart often. But I screamed at her, and let out all of the emotion at once. The sound echoed through the rooms as

Sara fled, scrambling away from the monster who was bleeding on the floor.

Sara

It was an hour before Rien came back. Or minutes, I don't know which. Time didn't work properly anymore, and my heart was beating so fast that I was sure I'd die of a heart attack before he came back to hurt me.

The look in his eyes... my God. I had no idea that anyone could have so much pain and anger. It was like a door had opened up to show me all of the horrible things inside of him, then swung back shut as quickly as he had opened. The grief on his face when he saw the globe broken... I would have done anything to take it back. I didn't know what he would do to me, but I knew that I had done something worse than I could understand.

When finally he came back into the library, I was sitting on the couch with the book in my lap–*Man's Search for Meaning*. I was trying to read it. Rather, my eyes moved back and forth over the same line again and again.

He looked haggard when he came back in. He slumped down in the corner near the end table, his eyes deadened. His hand was wrapped in cotton gauze, and the finger that he had cut blossomed red through the cotton.

He wasn't mad. That was the important thing. He didn't look like he was going to kill me. He just looked empty.

It was stupid to feel bad for him. I knew that. Gary had said that he was planning to kill me. He was a killer, a torturer. I knew that. I knew that, but it didn't matter right then, because of the emptiness that was in his face.

The emptiness that I created.

I struggled to find something to say to him. *I'm sorry* wouldn't cut it.

"That was your sculpture?" I asked finally.

"It was... yes. Yes." He snapped to attention, his eyes refocusing on me.

"I didn't mean to," I said, tears welling in my eyes. "Can I do anything to help?"

He shook his head slowly, his gaze turning to the bookshelves. He frowned.

"How did you know which book opened the secret door? I never let you see."

"I didn't."

"You tried them all to see which one would open it?"

"I just wanted something to read," I said. My hands cradled the book.

"Out of all the thousands of books on these shelves, you picked the one book that opened the doorway?" I shrugged helplessly.

His burst of laughter startled me. He leaned his head back against the bookshelves, rubbing his eyes with one hand.

"She just wanted something to read. That's... oh, Sara. I knew there was something about you."

Something about me? I didn't know what he was talking about, but when he looked over at me my skin grew hot. There was that predatorial look in his eyes again. That look that made me think he wanted to claim me. I touched my fingers to the page I was on.

"Why did you pick this book?" I asked.

"No reason."

I raised my eyebrows.

"You're telling me you picked a random book to cover the secret switch to your murder room?"

"No. I—" He stopped mid-sentence and peered

curiously at me. "Have you read it?"

"A long time ago," I said, thinking of my mother in the shelter. She'd turned the well-worn pages slowly. When I'd gotten the chance to read it, I'd flown through. Maybe I'd read it too quickly. I was too young to understand most of it.

Rien was staring ahead of him, his eyes becoming unfocused.

"There has to be a reason," I prodded. I wanted him back with me. Back in the present.

"You're right. Of course. There's a reason. There's a part... wait..."

He stood up slowly, being careful not to hurt his already-damaged hand. The few steps between us disappeared and his body sank into the cushions. Again, his shoulder brushed mine.

I shivered. He had been on the couch with me once before, and now my body reacted to his closeness as hotly as if he had put his hands on me. My pulse quickened and I swallowed back the sudden clench of desire that had wrapped itself around my throat.

Reaching over, he turned the pages of the book in my lap. His fingers were long, his hands strong. I thought of how he had touched me and closed my eyes. The smell of his cologne and the faint musk of his own body made me quicken with want. Desperate, I must be desperate to want this man. To want someone who plotted to murder me.

That's what Gary said. Now, sitting next to Rien, I couldn't believe that he'd been telling the truth. Not after I had seen Rien on the ground, shedding tears for a piece of art that I didn't understand. My whole body ached to comfort him. Yes, him, the murderer. He might be a killer, but he wasn't heartless.

"There," Rien said, and I caught myself from my thoughts. He was pointing to a line in the middle of the page. He began to read it, and I watched his lips move as he spoke softly.

"*If there is meaning in life at all, then there must be a meaning in suffering. Suffering is an ineradicable part of life, even as fate and death. Without suffering and death human life cannot be complete.*"

I realized as he finished speaking that I had been holding my breath. I let it out and tried to breathe normally.

"Do you believe in fate?" he asked. He looked into my eyes, and his nearness made me dizzy.

I thought of my mother and sister, and of how many times we had ended up sleeping in a shelter. Was I supposed to think that it was all for a good reason? I couldn't believe that.

"I don't think so," I said. "Do you?"

"Maybe. Sometimes I think things fall together for a reason. Even if it seems random."

"Like a desperate actress ending up locked in the library of a serial killer?"

"It must be for a reason. Fate must have a reason."

"Fate's kind of an asshole, then," I said.

"I don't consider myself a serial killer, anyway."

"Really? You kill people. That's kind of the definition of a serial killer, isn't it?"

"I'm more of an assassin."

"An assassin?"

"I work for the government. I'm not like some of my friends. I'm not a vigilante. They bring them to me. I know that they're bad people if they get to me."

"Are you going to assassinate me?"

I tried to ask it lightly, but he put his hands on my shoulders and turned me to face him.

"Sara, I am trying very hard to get you out of this. It's difficult. I'm not sure what I can do with you."

He didn't seem like he was lying. But then again, he

did this for a living. He lied to people and made them feel safe, and then he tortured them and killed them. He could sense my uncertainty and he brushed my cheek with his hand. His palm was warm against my skin. I struggled to keep my distance, to not fall forward to him. I felt like a complete idiot for trusting him but at the same time, I wanted to trust him with all my heart.

I gulped back the feeling. This was pretend. All pretend. But the walls were falling apart between the pretense and the reality, and I was falling for him, despite every rational thought that told me not to. Not the killer, but this man. The man who sat in front of me, tortured by his decisions. The man who could not kill me.

"I'm sorry that we met like this. I am. I want to see the real you. Not the actress. The real Sara."

He took my hands in his. I was tumbling forward into something I couldn't understand, something I couldn't accept, not with the logical part of my mind. I needed to pull back. I needed to distance myself from him.

I drew my hands back, out of his, and closed the book. I looked down at the cover.

"If there's a meaning in suffering, is that the meaning of your life? Causing people to suffer?"

"It's a steady gig."

A sudden jolt of anger pierced me. I didn't want this. The smooth-talking, cynical Rien. The Rien who killed and didn't care. I knew there was more to him than that, and now that I had seen it, I hated to have him close himself off to me again.

"You ask to see the real me. Then you joke. This isn't the real you, either," I said.

"You think you know the real me?" he asked. His voice was a low growl, but I was too upset to care about the danger.

"That's exactly it, Rien. I don't know the real you. I don't know you at all. I want to."

"Is that what you want?"

I nodded. I wanted to leave, and if I understood him, maybe I could convince him to let me go. Right now, I had no idea what was in his mind. More than that, I felt an irresistible need to understand why he did what he did. Why he had taken me, and touched me. Why he gave me pleasure, when all he gave to others was pain. Why he kept me here instead of killing me. If I understood him, I thought, I would have the upper hand.

He stood up and took the book from my hands. I waited silently as he walked to the bookshelf and replaced the book in the empty slot. With a click and a whir, the bookcase turned shut. Rien and I were alone in the library. The walls seemed to be closer than before. They loomed over us both. He came back and sat down on the couch, leaning toward me as though we were conspirators. I saw a glimmer of tears in his eyes again, just a flash, but then he blinked and the tears disappeared. He swallowed, his Adam's apple jerking sharply. Then he cleared his throat and spoke.

"Let me tell you about myself."

CHAPTER EIGHTEEN

Rien

I studied Sara's face. Her eyes were a brilliant green, sunk into pale hollows. She needed to go outside. She was like a flower who needed the sunshine, and would rot inside without it. I couldn't keep her here. And yet, I couldn't let her go without condemning us both. My heart was torn.

"You talk about suffering," I said. "But physical suffering is not the hardest kind to bear."

She turned up her face to me uncertainly. She didn't understand. Of course not. All she had had to bear was physical suffering. The cold of a nighttime without shelter. The ache of a stomach without food. The pain of a hand clamping down on her throat. My hand.

"I loved a girl once," I said.

"Who was she?"

"A young girl from another embassy. We were great friends. Her name was Michaela."

I breathed in. The room seemed stuffier than before, now that I'd closed the door. The air was thicker, like cotton.

"My family, though, didn't want us to be friends. They knew that our friendship was leading to love. And my mother especially couldn't stand to see me loving anything."

Sara frowned. Was I wrong to want to stop there? I couldn't. Not with her. Sara, of all the girls I'd ever met, was able to see past the surface evil. Maybe to actually see me. I couldn't hold back.

"My mother was evil. More evil than I turned out, maybe. Both of my parents hated to see me happy unless it was a happiness that they had given me. And they gave me everything. Everything I ever wanted. They gave me everything, but they took her away."

I closed my eyes, my breath shuddering through my body. I saw her face in my mind, her dark brown curls. The ache that always accompanied her memory ran through me like a blade. *Breathe, Rien.*

"Why?"

I clenched my jaw.

"Because she wasn't good enough for our family. They forbid me to play with her. They said her family was traitorous, that they were against what our country stood for. They were Communists, you see. And then one day my father came home and found us hiding in the attic, reading together. I couldn't disgrace our family name by loving someone from such a low family. From such a *disgraceful* family."

Sara's eyebrows knotted together on her forehead. Compassion filled her eyes. Was it true compassion? Nobody could have such compassion for a killer, and yet she looked at me without any trace of falseness.

"What happened?" she asked.

Could I trust her? I didn't know. There was something in her that made me want to. I had never told anyone this story before. I stood up and faced the bookshelf. When I spoke, my voice was even and calm.

"There was a raid on their embassy. It was to find an alleged traitor. They… they burned the building down. Her whole family was inside."

The brown curls, burning. Flames crawling through my memories. I closed my eyes.

"They didn't even burn it down themselves, you understand? They paid men to do it. Because they didn't want to get the filth on themselves. They wanted a perfect family, a perfect son who would do whatever they told him to do. But their hands were bloody, no matter what. They were evil, truly evil. When I kill those men on my table, I think of that kind of evil and I know what I'm doing is right."

I looked back at Sara. Tears ran down her cheeks. Alligator tears? I didn't know. I didn't care. I felt numb as I continued. She couldn't understand, but now that I was talking, I couldn't stop.

"So I ran away. I came here. And I kill people who want to escape from their evil pasts. For me, there is no escape. In my dreams, I see her burning."

I wet my lips.

"In some ways suffering ceases to be suffering at the moment it finds a meaning," I quoted. "My suffering didn't have a meaning before I took this job. But I take that suffering and I give it to others. It's the only trade that makes sense. It keeps me sane. And my life here is perfect. Or it was, before you."

"Me?"

I turned back to Sara. Her face, already pale, was paler now. Her tears still stained her cheeks.

"I'm falling apart because of you," I said.

She stood shakily from the couch and came to me. I reached out and cupped her cheek in my hand.

"I'm sorry," she said. She looked scared, so scared. Not as scared as I felt. My whole life that I had built up, all of the steadiness of my existence, was threatened because I couldn't kill her. I didn't know if what I felt was real. But I couldn't let myself be as evil as my family had been.

"Tell me what you want me to do," she whispered.

I touched her skin, brushing her beautiful dark locks away from her eyes and wiping the tears from her cheeks. Such depth in those eyes. I had taken her apart, but I couldn't put her back together. I broke everything I touched. It was all broken, all of it.

"I need to forget," I said. "I need you to want me."

"Rien…"

"Pretend to want me," I said. "You're good at that, aren't you?" I leaned forward and kissed her. Softly at first, then more deeply. Her full lips trembled against mine, and I pulled her body towards me. I wanted her. More than that, I wanted her desire. Even if it was fake. I didn't deserve more than that. I would take all that she offered, and more. She gasped as I kissed her, my mouth moving to her neck.

"Rien—"

"Pretend to love me. Can you do that, Sara?" I breathed against her neck, inhaling her scent, burying myself in her hair. My hands moved over her tense muscles, and where they went I felt her body melting towards me.

"Yes," she whispered. I kissed her again, her body leaning into mine. *The salvation of man is through love and in love.* This wasn't love. It wasn't real. But it was all I had, and even the shadow of love might be enough to keep the demons away.

Sara

Rien held me in his arms.

"Yes," I said. Pretend. Yes. I could pretend. My life had been a long pretense, a lesson in acting. This was just one more role.

And when he pulled me into his embrace, his lips crashing against mine, the aching desire that leapt up in my body was only pretend. That's what I told myself. I kissed him back, and the desperate need in his kiss spread the ache until every part of me wanted him against me.

His hands moved down my body, and my heart pounded as he kissed me again and again, his lips drawing new need from mine with every touch.

His hand brushed over my lower back, kneading my muscles as his lips took mine, sucking, licking. His hand moved down past the buttoned shirt and cupped my ass.

"Oh!" I cried out when his hand squeezed me there. My body clenched, and I felt the ache between my thighs give way to wetness. "Rien, please—"

He spun me, shoving me against the bookshelf. My breath left my body in one whoosh with the impact, and then he was kissing me again, kissing me so hard that it took all the rest of my breath from me. His body pressed against mine, pushing me hard against the shelves. He had me in his arms, pulling me up on tiptoe, and when he finally let go I gasped for air.

"I want you so badly," he whispered. I felt him against me, his thick erection straining through his pants. I imagined him filling me the way he had in the night, and my breath caught in my throat.

He'd taken me, and I'd liked it. And then he'd acted like it was nothing. Was this nothing, too? I couldn't believe it, not with the burning look of desire I saw in his eyes. When he'd taken me before, it had been completely dark. But maybe he was good at acting, better than I was. He'd asked me to pretend, and I would. Even if the pretense was only a thin veil that didn't mask what I really wanted. Wasn't that how the best actors did it, after all?

I shook myself free of my thoughts. I wanted nothing. This was only an act.

I reached up and pulled Rien in for another kiss. The hunger in his kisses shocked me and made the ache inside me grow. Then he grabbed my shirt with both hands and yanked. Buttons flew across the room as the fabric ripped apart. My body was exposed. His hands gripped my breasts so hard that tears sprung to my eyes. I moaned against his lips as he kissed me, his hands kneading my body.

His kisses moved down my neck to my shoulder. He bit down and I cried out. Immediately he relaxed his jaw, letting his teeth graze my collarbone. The edge of his teeth sent shivers through my bones.

"I need this," he mumbled against my skin. "Sara, forgive me. Forgive me."

My hands ran through his hair as he bent down to take my breast into his mouth. He sucked hard and I yelped, losing control of my muscles as the thrill ran through my body. If his hands hadn't been pressing me against the shelves, I would've fallen. He sucked my nipple, his teeth nipping the skin to make me cry out. I could tell he liked to hear me whimper, and I didn't try to hide my noises as he suckled me and teased my nipples with his tongue.

His mouth moved down, kissing the bare skin of my stomach. I jerked, but my hips only hit the shelves and he held me back so I could not move. My fingers gripped his hair. His tongue ran circles around the lower part of my stomach, pausing at the hipbone.

Was he? No. He wasn't. He couldn't.

"Rien—"

He tore my panties down with one hand, holding me up while I shifted my weight to let him take them off. I was dizzy with need. The ache inside of me was screaming for release, and I wanted him. God forgive me, I wanted him inside of me so badly. I could lie to anyone else, tell them that he had forced me, but in that moment I knew nothing but a primal need for him to satisfy me.

"Take me," I moaned. "I want you inside me, Rien."

"Not yet," he murmured. His face was pressed to my hip, his lips trailing down, down, and then—

"*OH!*" I cried out loud as he licked me once, hard, his tongue stoking the fire inside of me to unbelievable heights. My muscles turned to rags, and I screamed as he buried his face between my thighs. His tongue licked me in long, slow strokes, so slow that they tore my nerves to pieces and left me shaking with desire. I needed more, more, but every time I came close he only eased off and left me wanting.

"Rien, please. Oh God, Rien. Don't stop." I was babbling, my hands grabbing his hair and pulling his head back towards me. He pressed kisses all along the outside of my folds. I was burning, burning. I would die if he did not touch me again.

"Tell me you want me, Sara."

"I want you. Please."

"Tell me you love me."

"I—I—"

My voice choked. I could not say the words and I did not know why. His command had closed down something inside of me.

His mouth sealed over me, and I screamed as he sucked my swollen clit, licked it hard and sent me soaring for a split second before he pulled away.

"Rien!"

"Tell me!" His voice was a growl, an order, full of a terrible need that sent a darkness into my heart.

"I— love you."

I forced the words out. Once they were in the air, I felt as though I'd done something wrong. Before, I might have been pretending, but this felt worse, somehow. I'd lost something between us, something I didn't understand.

His mouth was on me again. It sent all of my thoughts into a whirlwind of varying brightness. The walls of the room spun around me as his tongue circled my aching, tender clit. My body began to rock forward against his mouth. He flicked me with his tongue, and I gasped, my hips jerking forward involuntarily. His arms wrapped around my thighs, holding me back against the shelves.

"Oh yes, Rien," I cried out. His mouth sealed again around my swollen clit, his tongue probing me greedily. The shudder began to rise inside of me, and I tangled my fingers in his hair, pulling him harder against me. My heart pounded in my ears.

"*Yes! Yes! YES!*"

I screamed as the orgasm tore through my nerves. I held onto his shoulders for dear life, knowing I would collapse to the floor if he did not hold me up. Fireworks exploded from my core and the room turned a blinding white as wave after wave of my climax crashed through my body. And still his tongue was working circles around me, pulling every scrap of pleasure from my body as I came, screaming, screaming as though it was pain and not pleasure that shot through my whole being. I gushed, the orgasm sending me over the edge and into an abyss that I doubted I could ever escape from.

I shuddered once, then again, my hips bucking against his mouth, as the pleasure rolled through me. The room still swayed, or was that my body? I trembled, and my fingers slowly relaxed. Rien's tongue stroked me slowly, his breath cool against my hot slick skin. Softly, softly, he pressed a kiss against me, sending one more shudder through me.

He stood up, and I could feel his hardness against my thigh as he held me up.

"Rien," I whispered, my voice hoarse. He kissed me on the forehead, brushing back my hair.

Then he grabbed me with both hands and threw me against the back of the couch. I stumbled and fell. My hands dug into the cushions. He grabbed my shoulder and shoved his leg against my inner thigh, pushing me forward even more. Bending me over the couch. He leaned close to me, his breath in my ear, and what he said made me shiver with as much fright as desire.

"You're mine now."

CHAPTER NINETEEN

Rien

I couldn't stop. Her taste was on my tongue. I pulled her away from the bookshelves and spun her back toward the couch.

She was mine. Mine. I couldn't control the savage lust inside of me. I bent her over the couch. Her soft cries, her needy noises, the sound of her breath catching as I forced her over the cushions–they drove me to a need that I'd never experienced before.

Mine.

I had to have her. My hands moved along her creamy skin. Her perfect hips pressed against the couch. My hand wrapped around her neck and kneaded the muscles there. I savored her small gasps as I worked my way between her legs, my fingers ripping at the button of my fly. My cock was throbbing in my hand as I took it out.

"*Ohh!*" she cried out as I pressed the tip to her soaking wet slit. I couldn't wait. No. I kicked her legs apart and she opened to take me.

Pink, perfect. I ran my hands over her asscheeks, my thumbs brushing the edges of her slick folds. She moaned and my cock pulsed at the sound. I paused at her entrance, letting the tip of my cock trace a delicious circle around her.

"Please," she cried. "Please."

I spanked her hard and she gasped, jerking backwards against me. My legs had her pinned and she couldn't move. I spanked her again and my handprint rose red like a blush on her pale ass. Her rippling curves were too much. I was trying to keep myself from coming right then and there.

Pretend, I said to her. She was quite the actress. As I thrust forward, her body closed in around my shaft, clenching tight around me. God, I could feel her muscles working my cock from tip to base. I bit my lip, raising my hand to spank her again. At the slap, I could feel her body tense around me, then loosen. Again. Tense, then loose. Again.

My balls tightened as I rocked back, then forward, working my aching cock deep into her. I couldn't last long, I knew. Eating her sweetness had gotten me so hot that I thought a single thrust would have been enough to tip me over the edge. Now, though, I couldn't stop until I was done with her completely. I wanted her to be mine. I didn't want it to end, and I fought the pressure that built up in my balls and my throbbing shaft.

I fucked her hard, angling into her so that I could penetrate her completely. Again and again I rocked forward, her thighs banging against the couch with every thrust.

Her cries grew louder and louder as I fucked her harder. Sweat ran down my neck and slicked my hands on her skin. Delicious friction. Tender, tight flesh. And a woman whose curves I could not stop squeezing, spanking, caressing. I held her hips tightly as I slammed into her over and over again from the back, pumping hard. The tense pressure in me built as I jackhammered my swollen thickness deep into her.

Her cries grew faster and higher-pitched, and then she was climaxing again, the tops of her knees hitting the back of the couch. I buried myself inside her. My balls ached for release.

She screamed. Her fingers scrabbled against the

couch cushions as she pushed herself back onto me to impale herself onto my cock. Her climax vibrated against me, and it took me over the top. With one hard thrust I released inside of her. Stars exploded as her body clenched my shaft, milking every drop from my cock and sending me into shudders against her body. I jerked once, twice, then settled against her body with my hands on her back.

"*Sara*," I whispered.

The emotion that came over me was unsettling. I'd ordered her to pretend, and she had. I'd told her to say that she loved me, and she had. I'd thought that all of it meant nothing. But now, holding her shaking body underneath mine, I knew that I couldn't go back. I'd done something worse to her than to any of my victims. Rather than drawing the truth from her with pain, I'd forced her to fake pleasure.

I felt a deep sense of unease. *Was* she faking? Did she fake all of it? I didn't know, and the not knowing is what killed me.

False love was no love. No, it was worse than that. She was my toy, and I'd ruined her.

My stomach churned as I withdrew from her body. Such beauty, but it was not mine. I could no longer tell what was real and what was fantasy. Her love was fantasy. Her fear was real. Or was it the other way around?

I needed to know, but I couldn't ask her. Letting my hands fall from her body, I stepped back shakily and opened the bookcase.

"Rien?" She leaned against the back of the couch and her face turned to look at me. She was pale, scared.

Was that what I had done to her?

"I'm sorry," I said, and turned away. I had created a dream, but I couldn't live in it forever.

Sara

Rien looked as though he'd seen a ghost. He fumbled with his pants, pulling them back up around his waist as he walked back into the operating room. The bookcase spun shut behind him.

I didn't understand what had just happened. My hands trembled against the couch cushions. I slid down the back of the couch to the floor and huddled there. My arms wrapped around my legs even though I wasn't cold.

"Think, Sara," I whispered to myself. "Think. Don't feel. Just think."

Rien was planning to kill me. I had to take it from there. If he planned to kill me, then this was all a game. He was toying with me before he killed me. He was a cat playing with a mouse. He was using me for fun, for sex, before he strapped me down and had fun with me in other ways.

I shook my head. Something about that idea didn't seem right to me. Maybe it was the way he held me in his arms and kissed me so tenderly, but I simply couldn't believe that he was plotting to murder me

"Come on, Sara," I said, frowning. "Of course it doesn't seem like it. He's good at lying to you."

That's it. That's all it was. He was lying to me.

I swallowed hard. I didn't want to think about his hands, his tongue, his mouth on my body... as lies. Because as much as he might have been pretending, my body's responses were all real. My emotions were all true.

Even the ones I couldn't admit.

I pulled the shirt back over my chest. The buttons were mostly ripped off, but a couple still hung on. I buttoned what I could. I found my panties bunched up next to the bookcase. They were wet anyway. I didn't have any other clothes.

I rested my head on my knees to try to calm myself down. My heart still pounded from my orgasm. It was a horrible thought, but I wanted Rien back. I wanted him to hold me again. Stupid, a stupid feeling, but I wanted him to care about me. I didn't want to believe that he was only pretending. I didn't want to believe that what had just happened was only a scene that we'd both acted in.

"No, Sara." I shook my head. "No, no, no."

I'd heard all of the stories about method actors. How Daniel Day Lewis had been playing the role of a crazy person and had gone crazy himself after spending days depriving himself of sleep. There were dozens of couples who had started out acting opposite one another in movies. Their characters fell in love, and they followed suit in real life. It was such a cliché, but it was true.

Delsarte knew that. He was one of the first people in theatre to propose the idea that emotions follow from facial expressions. If you frown, he said, you start to become angry. If you smile, you start to become happy. This was a couple hundred years ago, but even today you could see that concept all over the place.

There was a psychological study that had a bunch of people watch a comedy show. One group held a pencil above their upper lip so that they were forced to bare their teeth, like a smile. That group always found the comedy show funnier than the group who hadn't been forced to smile.

Another study found that people who flexed their muscles and posed like Superman before an interview tended to do much better than people who were forced to do timid poses, like bending over and clutching their knees. Delsarte might not have been a method actor, but he knew something about psychology.

I looked down at my own posture. My arms were wrapped around my knees, in just about the most timid, un-Superman like pose ever.

"Okay, Sara," I said, pushing myself up. I stood up on trembling legs. "Let's become a survivor. Okay? Okay."

I stood with my feet apart, and I flexed my arms like Mr. America. I didn't feel strong, though. I felt utterly stupid.

I tried another pose, hands on my hips, chest out. Okay. Better. I was feeling my fright drain away. This could actually work. Thank you, Delsarte. I stretched my arms out and made a monster face, growling.

"I am the monster," I said, making myself as big as possible. "I am strong. I am a survivor. I—"

CRASH!

The noise came from behind the bookcase. Was it Gary? Or Rien? I froze for a moment, not sure what I should do. Then I took a deep breath and shook the remainder of my fears away. Whatever it was, I could handle it. I stepped to the bookcase and pulled out *Man's Search for Meaning*, not sure what I would find behind the door when it opened.

CHAPTER TWENTY

Sara

I stepped into the operating room, my eyes darting from side to side. Rien was nowhere to be seen. I heard another crash.

It came from the waiting room.

I ran to the doorway and stopped there, frozen in the doorway, unable to believe what I was seeing.

The metal stool was in Rien's hand. He'd smashed both of the mirrored walls in the waiting room. He stood in the middle of the room with the broken glass globe at his feet. The shattered mirrors reflected his face a thousand different ways. His face was as white as the tiles in the operating room.

"Sara?" The question was hoarse and unsteady. He looked around the room in confusion, as though unsure if he had done all of this himself. His reflections splintered in the broken glass.

"What are you doing?" I asked.

"It was too much," he said. The metal stool clanged noisily to the ground. He waved a hand at the broken mirrors. "All of this. Too much."

"I don't understand," I said. He looked up at me like I'd interrupted him.

"It's all fake, all of it. The mirrors, they lie. They don't tell the truth." He talked like an insane person, running both hands through his hair as he muttered.

"Rien, I don't—"

"You don't understand! That's why!" he yelled.

Then his voice softened. "It's me, Sara. I'm sorry. It's me. Come, let me tell you something."

I stepped forward nervously. I didn't know what to expect when I came through the door, but it wasn't this. Rien seemed angry, but not at me. He looked angrily at the mirrors and at the broken glass. He took my hands in his and knelt down, pulling me down next to him. I sat on the floor, in the one clean patch of tile that didn't have shards of glass. He held both of my hands, his palms hot against mine.

"Have you ever heard of a delusion called Capgras syndrome?"

"Cap—what?"

"Capgras. Never mind the name. Names mean nothing. Nothing, right?"

"Right," I said dizzily.

"It's a disorder I learned about in medical school, during an elective course in neuropsychology. It's a problem between the thinking part of your brain and the emotional part of your brain."

I furrowed my brow and listened closely even though I didn't understand what exactly he was talking about. He looked so upset, his eyes frantic.

"The delusion comes when you look at another person, someone you know. If you have Capgras syndrome, you can recognize someone, but there's something wrong when you look at them. You feel like they're an impostor, or a robot. Something that doesn't have the same emotions as the person you used to know. You recognize their outside, but their inside is gone, disappeared. They're not themselves."

"That's... that's a thing? A real disease?" I couldn't believe it.

"One woman claimed that her husband had been replaced by an identical copy of his body in the middle of the night. She wouldn't sleep with him; she locked him out of the house. Because she couldn't recognize him as the same person he was before. Another man claimed that everybody in the world was a robot but him."

"What's wrong with them?"

Rien seized my head in his hands with a sudden jerk and I gasped. He leaned close so that his face was only inches from mine.

My pulse rate jumped up. He looked deep into me, his anger replaced by sadness.

"What's wrong with us, Sara? I think I know, but I'm not sure."

"You have this thing? This… this syndrome?" Was that why sorrow drew his face tight?

I could feel his breath on my lips when he answered. His scent was salty, like the ocean, with only a hint of cologne. My heart raced.

"I don't know. Maybe. It comes in flashes, not always. Sometimes I can tell when a person is lying. There's a screen over them, like a mask that only I can see. And sometimes it feels like they don't even exist, that's how much they're pretending. Maybe everybody in the world is really fake."

Rien tilted his head, looking at me first at one eye, then the other. He peered into me like he was trying to see something. His fingers gripped my hair.

"Am *I* fake?" I gulped. "Do you think I'm fake?"

"I don't know, Sara. I don't know." His fingers relaxed, and I exhaled slowly. "Sometimes I think you are, and then I look again and I see something so vulnerable that it must be real. Everybody pretends sometimes. It's the people who think they're not pretending who are the real liars."

I waited for a moment, thinking about all the lies I'd told in the past year. If I had to go to confession, it would take hours. I couldn't judge Rien.

"What about you?" I asked.

"Me?"

I breathed in, biting my lip.

"Are you lying to me?"

He let me go. I rocked back on my knees, trying to catch my breath. His intensity took all of the air out of the room.

"Maybe. Sometimes, when I look in the mirror, I don't know what's looking back. I don't know who I'm becoming."

"You mean, you think you're the impostor?"

"I don't know," he said sadly. He turned toward the mirrored wall. His face reflected back in myriad broken pieces, flashed through the glass shards on the floor. "Maybe I'm not real. I look at myself but there's nothing looking back. Sometimes. I've learned to live with it, but..."

He trailed off, his eyes glazing over.

I thought of something. I cleared my throat and he turned back to me.

"You asked me before what made me want to be an actress. What made you want to do this?"

"What made me want to kill? What made me want to murder people?" He looked right at me when he said it.

"Yes."

"It started... it started when I got my first client from the federal witness protection program. Vale came to talk with me before the surgery."

Vale? I must have looked at him questioningly, because he explained.

"My boss. He's the liaison between the government and the people who do the government's dirty work. If you think I'm bad... well, he's been doing this longer than I have. He sent me this client. I didn't know it at the time, but he was feeling me out for this job. He asked me if I'd be willing to do plastic surgery on a criminal, if I could keep my mouth shut."

"The client, he was a mob guy. He needed multiple plastic surgeries before leaving for Canada. I met him the first time, and he was a horrible person. Just horrible. He talked about all of the crimes he'd committed. He talked to me about killing a rival's family, the wife, the children. One of them a baby. He laughed when he said he would get away with them all.

"I guess Vale told him that he could talk freely around me. Looking back on it, Vale probably goaded him to brag about his crimes in order to make me sick about it. Then, before his last appointment, Vale came to me and told me that he wanted me to kill the mob guy. To make him disappear, was how he put it. He said that if I didn't want to do it, he could get someone else to do it. Then he told me what he'd pay."

"He offered you a lot of money, I bet."

Rien laughed a cold laugh.

"Sure. You see where I live, don't you? You see the view from out there. The U.S. government pays its people well. But that wasn't why I did it."

"It wasn't?"

"I did it because after talking with him, I hated him. I hated that he was going to be able to run away and start over. I hated that this man, this killer, would be out there free and living well, while good people starved on the streets. It wasn't fair. It wasn't right. I wanted to do it, you see? I wanted to kill him. And not just kill. I wanted to torture him, to make him pay."

His eyes were bright and animated as he spoke. The irises shone like tiger's eye.

"And once I'd killed him, I didn't want to stop. I asked Vale, I remember..." he trailed off, staring blankly into the air. "I asked him in a roundabout kind of way. I remember being nervous that he would say no. But of course he wanted me to work for him. He set me up with all of his clients from then on. And it was beautiful. I felt like it was what I was meant to do. *Man's main concern is not to gain pleasure or to avoid pain but rather to see a meaning in his life.* And that was my meaning."

He closed his eyes, breathing deeply. I didn't know what to say to him. I didn't know what he wanted me to say. Here, sitting next to him in a room full of broken glass and mirrors, I was lost in his confusion. So instead, I wrapped my arms around him. I hugged him, this monster, this killer. I hugged him tightly, knowing that he might kill me next. I hugged him because there was nothing else I could do to help and I needed to help him, God only knows why. Because there was something in him that kindled a strange desire, and I had spent my life suppressing my desires. Here, though, there was no reason to hold back.

Rien was better than me, because he knew what he wanted. His life was real, full of real actions and real consequences. I had spent all of my life pretending. I envied him, in a strange, dark way. I wanted to know what it was like to have that kind of power. To have that kind of meaning.

A moment passed, and he sat back, trembling.

"What happened, then?" I said.

He looked at me, tilting his head. Not understanding.

"You said you had found your meaning." I looked around the room, at the broken mirrors, the shards of glass. "What happened? What happened here?"

"Oh, Sara," he said. His hands moved to my face, caressing my cheeks. "My dear, my dear."

In a thousand different reflections, tears fell from his eyes, twinkling in the low light. He cupped my cheeks and leaned in to me, pressing his forehead against mine in such an intimate pose that I forgot where we were for a moment. His voice was so low that it was almost inaudible.

"You happened."

Rien

"Me?"

The girl was beautiful, beautiful and lost at the same time. I could see it in her face, in the slight tremble of her hands. How did she get here? I looked around my waiting room. The walls were spiderwebs of cracks. The mirrors reflecting our sad faces. Scattered at our feet were all the plastic pieces, the reminders of my other victims.

"You're not real," I said. "You're beautiful and perfect and not real. I don't know what to do now that I've had a taste of you."

"I'm real," she said. Her lip quivered.

"You are an actress. It's what you do. You pretend, and you pretend beautifully. But nothing you've done here is real."

"No," she said. Her voice was firmer. "No, that's not true."

"No? Would you have done all this, if I hadn't asked you to? If a killer hadn't ordered you to kiss him, would you have done it?"

"I flirted with you before I knew you were a killer," she said. She was unsteady.

"And after you knew? Did you want me? Not just because I told you to?"

She tilted her face up to me. Her eyelashes fluttered.

"Yes," she said quietly.

"I wish I could believe you," I said.

"Why don't you?" She frowned. "I'm telling you now. There's no reason for me to lie."

"There are always reasons to lie," I said, waving my

hand in irritation. "But it wouldn't have to be a lie. I have too much first-hand experience with Stockholm Syndrome."

"Is that what you think this is?"

"Isn't it?" My voice grew louder as anger swept through me. I wanted her. I'd confided to her. And it made me irrationally mad to think that she wasn't real. It made me even angrier to hear her deny it. "Don't tell me you're not acting."

"How can I prove that? How can I do anything but tell you I'm not lying?" She sounded as frustrated as I felt.

I blinked. Proof. Vale needed proof. So did I. I had an idea. Crazy, maybe. But it would help narrow my options. Jake still hadn't called me back about Susan Steadhill, and time was running out. I was uncertain about Sara, but maybe I didn't need to be.

"Come here," I said. I offered a hand to her, pulling her up from the ground. She stood, and I realized that she wasn't wearing any panties. She needed something to change into.

Yes. That would be fine. That would be just fine.

"Come with me," I said, pulling her hand. I might be crazy. It might not work. But maybe it would.

"Where are we going?" she said.

"We're going to have a date," I said.

CHAPTER TWENTY-ONE

Sara

Rien wouldn't tell me what he was doing. A date? I had no idea what he meant by that. In the operating room, he pulled out a length of cotton gauze. When he turned to me with it, I gulped.

"Don't worry," he said. "I'm not going to gag you."

"Then what—"

"Turn around."

I obeyed, and his hands pulled the cotton gauze over my eyes. His fingers knotted the gauze at the back of my head. Everything was white and fuzzy.

"I don't trust you yet," he said, his voice close to my ear. "But maybe I will be able to."

A frightened thrill ran through me. His hand pressed on my lower back and I let him lead me out. We stepped through to the library, and I heard the bookcase close. Then I heard a metal bolt click, and the creak of the oak door. The floor was cold under my feet.

"We're going into your house?" I asked.

"I don't let anyone back here," he said.

"Is that because it's so messy you have to blindfold people to walk them through the house?"

"No," he said. "I don't want you seeing any points of exit."

"Right. Because you don't trust me yet."

"And because I want to do something to you."

"Wait, what?"

I stumbled, and he caught me. He held me steady,

his hand soft but firm, guiding. I felt the texture of the floor change under my feet as we moved from the hardwood floor of the library to tile. My hand clutched his upper arm, relying on him to lead me.

"*Do something* to me?"

"I won't hurt you tonight, Sara."

"Alright." That didn't really give me much comfort. Whether or not he hurt me tonight didn't mean anything if he planned to kill me tomorrow. But I supposed I could take it one step at a time.

We made it into a darkened room, and when he turned the light on, all I could see was a white haze. Then I heard water running.

"A shower?"

"You have to get ready for our date," Rien said.

"Can I take this gauze off?"

"Absolutely not. Not yet, anyway."

Rien let go of me for a moment. I heard a clink and a shuffle of fabric. Then his hands were on my shoulders, pulling back the torn shirt. I let him take off the ripped remainder of my clothing. I stood there naked, with only a blindfold of cotton gauze. The chill of the air stiffened my nipples almost instantly, and I crossed my arms in front of my chest. My heart raced.

I don't know what made me so nervous. Rien had seen me naked before, of course. He'd done a lot more to me already than he was about to do. But I couldn't help but shiver in anxious anticipation as I stood blindly in the middle of his bathroom. Maybe it was that I couldn't see a damn thing. Even Rien was only a shadow moving on the white cotton covering my eyes.

"Here you go," Rien said. His hand touched my lower back and I jumped. "It's alright. I'll lead you."

I felt the steam coming off of the shower before I stepped in. I moaned in pleasure as I ducked under the water stream. God, the hot water felt good. It had only been what, two days since I had taken a shower? I leaned back and let the water flow through my hair.

"I foresee a problem with your plan, Rien," I called out.

"What's that?"

"How am I going to shampoo my hair with this blindfold on?"

In response, the lights in the bathroom went out. I blinked behind my blindfold in astonishment. The white cotton gauze had taken away my vision, sure, but now everything had gone *dark*. It was a totally different kind of blindness.

"You can take the blindfold off now," Rien said. His voice was right outside, and as I pulled off the cotton gauze, I heard him come into the shower. The door closed with an audible *click*. Then his hand touched me on the stomach and I yelped.

"Sorry," he said, and although it was totally dark, I could tell that he was smiling at me. "Just trying to orient myself." His hand touched my shoulder, and I could sense him moving around to my back. The shower was big, but not that big, and his hand stayed on my shoulder as he moved.

"Why are you making me take a shower in the dark, again?" I asked. "Because there really aren't any exit points in here, unless you count the drain, and I'm not escaping down that way."

"Oh, I just like taking showers in the dark," Rien said. Again, I could see his smile without seeing it. "I thought you would enjoy it, too."

"I think I need to be able to see my body to know if I'm clean or not," I said.

"Don't worry," Rien said. "I'll make sure every inch of you is clean."

His hand smoothed my shoulder and I felt a bar of soap sliding across my back. He rubbed the soap over my skin. True to his word, he didn't leave a single place untouched. At my shoulders, his hands kneaded, massaging me. I let out a sigh as I felt my tensions melting away. Not all of my tensions, of course. This was a murderer who was giving me a shoulder rub in the shower; I wasn't about to forget that. But most of them.

His other hand came around my front with the bar of soap. I gasped as I felt his chest press against my back. He slid the soap across my stomach, then up between my breasts. I moaned as he rubbed my breasts, his hands slippery and hot, fondling, stroking, cupping and squeezing. His fingers slid in a slow pinch around my nipples, twisting slightly until I cried out, then letting go. I could hear his breath against my ear as he continued to squeeze, and his cock stiffened against my back.

"I... I think the girls are clean by now, Rien."

"You can never be too sure."

Was that a joke? Was he joking? His moods were so variable. I couldn't tell what was pretend and what was real.

His hand slid down between my thighs. Slippery with soap, he stroked me up and down, cleaning me in areas only I'd ever touched. In the darkness, I felt his hands, his chest, his cock.

"Tilt your head back," he said. His hand was on my chin. I let him guide me under the stream of hot water, letting the warmth flow through my hair. Then his hands came up and I felt him rubbing shampoo into my hair in slow circles. His fingers ran across my scalp, sending thrills down my spine. One hand came forward, encircling my throat. I breathed in sharply and he held my throat as calmly and steadily as he had before. *Mine*, he told me with his hands. *You're mine.*

The other hand continued to lather as he tortured me with gentle squeezes. My breath hitched as his fingernails sent electrical pulses through my skull. He held my head in his hands like he was one of those quacks who study phrenology, studying the bumps on my head with his fingertips. He smoothed conditioner over my wet hair, his fingers untangling the mess slowly, patiently. Everything about him was patient. It felt like it had been forever since I had been in the shower.

Dark, so dark. I closed my eyes and imagined his face. His eyes sparkling with gold flecks. His sharp jaw, the dark stubble defining his chin. The soft dark locks hanging down to his brow. His hands moved, sliding over my head, my throat, back to my shoulders.

He turned me so that I was facing sideways. My fingers brushed his erection and I heard him take a sharp inward breath. His reaction was an unbelievable turn on. Then he leaned forward and his whisper made my heart flutter.

"Touch me," he said.

I let my fingers find their way along his shaft, stroking lightly. As I touched him, his hands continued to caress my arms, my back, my stomach with soap. His cock jumped in my hand and I bit my lip. His desire ignited mine, like nothing else had done before. The darkness enveloped us, closing around us with warm water and steam and the fresh scent of soap.

Then his hand curved around my ass, circling back. I whimpered as his fingers slid down, touching me in the back. I froze, my hand squeezing the base of his cock, as his fingers ran lightly across my pucker. Slippery, probing.

"Rien—"

"Is this new to you?"

All of it, I wanted to say. This was all new to me. My previous love affairs had been dreary and one-dimensional. Other actors, who acted in the bedroom as they would have acted in a love scene, cameras rolling.

Never anything new, never anything real. Sex like they were reading their blocking from a script.

But this… this was real. Exciting. Terrifying. His fingers thrilled me, and I moved my hand along his length, wanting to give back to him what he had given to me. He pulled me against him tightly, his hand still exploring me. In the darkness, I could hear his heartbeat begin to quicken.

My asshole was burning with sensation as his fingertip moved in circles over the puckered flesh. Every nerve of mine fluttered when he paused at my entrance. Then he pushed inside, just a bit, and I gasped with shock. Stars burst in the black air of the shower and I clutched his other arm with my free hand to keep from falling.

"Sara," he murmured. His finger pushed in, then withdrew. Pushed in, then withdrew. I cried out. The sensation was like nothing else I had ever felt before. The strange feeling of his finger probing me, expanding me. The nerves that had never been touched like this by anyone else. Then he withdrew completely, and I whimpered, my hand closing around his cock.

He took my hand in his and pressed it between his palms.

"Finish showering and come out to the bedroom," he said, kissing me lightly on the forehead. Water streamed down between our bodies. "If you need a razor, there's one by the soap dish. I'm going to get some things ready." The shower door opened, and I felt a burst of cool air come in from the bathroom.

"The blindfold?" I asked. My thoughts were whirling. He was leaving me with a razor. Did that mean he trusted me?

"No," he said. "You've been very good. You may leave it off. But don't go wandering around."

"Thank you," I said.

As he left the bathroom, he flicked a switch and a dim light came on. After the total darkness, it was like being illuminated by the sun. Rien's shadow passed over the doorway, and then he was gone.

I looked all around me, taking in my surroundings. The shower was a cream marble tile, and there was a razor exactly where he'd said it would be. He'd left a towel hanging over the glass door of the shower. I smoothed shaving cream over my legs and shaved quickly.

He trusted me. He trusted me. The thought pounded in my mind as I finished cleaning up. My stomach was in knots. Why was I so worried? I'd been on a thousand bad dates before. A date with a serial killer… well, how bad could it be?

I rinsed, turned off the shower, and toweled myself off. Stepping out of the bathroom, I saw a dress lying on the bed. It was a strapless evening gown, green with gold beading at the waist. There was a note lying next to it.

Dress up for me. Then wait here.

I picked up the dress, touching the silk fabric in wonder. He must have gotten my size from the dress I'd been wearing when I first arrived.

Two days ago. That was it. Two days in this place, and I felt like another person. As I pulled the dress over my head and adjusted it on my hips, I wondered what Rien was doing to me. Looking in the mirror, I tried to see myself as I looked now. Was I an impostor? Or was I more real now? My heart was beating fast as I combed my hair out with my fingers. I wanted Rien to see me, to think that I was beautiful. I wanted him to hold me, to take me, to—

"What's happening to me?" I asked my reflection. She didn't answer. Neither one of us knew if the world we were living in was real.

Rien

I whistled as I reduced the sauce in the steak pan. The night had been fragmented, but I had come up with an idea that I was certain would work. This would be the final test, and then I would have to decide.

Jake still hadn't contacted me, and Vale would expect me to have the proof ready for him tomorrow. If I could trust her, then things would be easy. If not...

Well, I didn't want to think about that.

I set dinner up in front of the fireplace in the main room. That's right, the fireplace. Every mansion in Hollywood has a fireplace, as if we all agreed to reject the reality that Southern California is hot and humid year-round. I lit the fire and adjusted the tablecloth on the small table. No candle, just firelight. Perfect.

When I went to get her, she was sitting on the bed. I wanted to throw her back and ravish her right then. Her eyes sparkled green, the color matching her dress perfectly. She blushed when I told her how beautiful she looked. Everything was stupidly perfect. If I wasn't supposed to kill her by tomorrow night, I would be utterly relaxed.

"You made me dinner?" she asked. "I don't think anyone's made me dinner before."

"Your mom never made you dinner?"

"She was always working," Sara said, her face expressionless. I wanted to pull her out from behind that mask, and let her know that she could be her true self around me. Flaws and all.

I guided her to the main room and pulled out the chair for her. A gentleman killer. I poured her a glass of wine and touched my glass to hers.

"To your health," I said.

"Very funny."

"I'm sorry. I didn't mean—"

"How can you do this?"

"Excuse me?" I tucked my napkin over my lap.

"I don't understand," she said. "How can you kill these people?"

"I told you," I said, spearing a carrot with my fork. "The people I kill are murderers themselves, or worse. It's a relief to me and a relief to society."

"And the police don't care?"

I couldn't help but chuckle.

"The Feds sweep it all under the rug. Vale handles his business well."

"Vale?"

"My boss. Look. It's my job. That's all. That's what happens with a job. You just shut up and do what has to be done."

"Do what has to be done?"

"They're murderers, Sara. And they're cowardly murderers at that."

"What do you mean, cowardly?"

"Like Mr. Steadhill in there. They murder indirectly. They don't get their hands dirty. They're afraid of dirty work."

"And you're not."

"Me, I get the job done."

"Except this one?"

She stared across the table at me, taunting me with her stare. As though she wouldn't be dead already if I hadn't spared her. Her emerald eyes bored a hole through me. I longed to kiss her again, to gaze into her eyes as I brought her to pleasure. And then, as though reading my stare, her eyelashes fluttered downward.

"You're right," I said, my voice dark with everything I wanted to say and couldn't. "Except this one."

CHAPTER TWENTY-TWO

Rien

"You have a fireplace," Sara noted. "That's strange."

"Why is it strange?"

"What you told me about when you were a kid. And that girl."

"You think I should be afraid of fire?"

"Well…"

"There isn't anything I'm more afraid of," I said. "But fear is one of the most primal emotions. When I'm afraid, I'm awake. You can't run away from things you're afraid of."

A moment passed. The flames danced in her eyes.

"I wish—"

She cut off her sentence, and I took her hand in mine across the small table. She looked up at me with a gleam of tears in her eyes.

"What is it?" I asked.

"I wish this wasn't a prison. I wish I had met you somewhere else."

"If you had met me somewhere else, I wouldn't have seen the real you, would I?"

"No. No, I suppose not." She cast her eyes downwards. "Have you decided what you're going to do with me?"

"I'm working on it."

She bit her lip, and I wanted to hold her and tell her that it would all be fine. But of course I didn't know if it would be.

"Sara, I need to ask you something."

"Yes?"

She looked up hopefully.

"You talked with Mr. Steadhill about his wife."

The fire in her eyes died. She swallowed another sip of wine, but I could still see the disappointment in her face. I hated to disappoint her. Hopefully, after tonight, I wouldn't have to.

"Yes," she said.

"Did you ever meet her?"

"No."

"Do you know where she is?"

"Susan? No. I have no idea."

"What else did he say to you about her?"

"We just talked about what she was like. How she acted. So that I could act like her."

"Did he mention her going anywhere? Maybe in hiding?"

"No. I didn't even know they were in the witness protection program until he told you," Sara said. She shifted in her seat. "He said they had been fighting."

"Maybe another house she owns? A favorite hotel?"

Sara looked up at me, her eyes narrowing.

"I don't know where Susan Steadhill is," she repeated flatly.

I sighed. I leaned back in my chair and downed the rest of my wine. It frustrated me beyond end to not have any leads. I didn't know whether I hoped that she was telling me the truth or if I hoped she was lying. If she was lying, then there was still a possibility I could find Susan tomorrow before Vale came. If not...

"Why do you care?"

I shook myself out of my reverie.

"I need to give them teeth."

"Teeth?" Her voice rose in disbelief.

"Proof, I mean. Teeth are proof. I was supposed to

kill her. I need to find her. I need to kill her. That bastard on the table says she's in Brazil."

"So are you going to go to Brazil?"

"No. I don't believe him."

"Why not?"

"Because if she left for Brazil already, the feds would have been on it. They wouldn't have let you walk through my door. They would have known you weren't her."

"So she's still in L.A.," Sara said, her eyes narrowing.

"That's my guess. Pretending to be someone else."

She let out a breath, and I licked my lips. If she was lying, she was damn good at it. But I had to be sure.

It was time.

"Wait here a moment," I said. I went to the other room and brought back the dessert I had bought earlier.

"A cupcake!" she exclaimed. "Oh, with raspberries. That's my favorite!"

"I'm glad," I said. "It's soaked in a raspberry brandy coulis. I made that separate."

"Delicious," she said, forking a mouthful to her lips. "Thank you."

"Of course. I wanted tonight to be special."

I watched her eat, bite by bite. Once she was finished, she took another sip of wine, swallowing. I stood up and put another log into the fire.

"Rien—"

I turned. Her eyes glazed over.

"*The real strong have no need to prove it to the phonies*," I said. "That's Charles Manson. Unfortunately, Sara, I'm not that strong. I need proof."

"What… what do you…"

"I need to trust you. Wholly. Completely. And there's only one way I know of to do that."

"Rien, I don't—I feel..."

She stood up from the table, her hand reaching out to steady herself. She knocked over the wine glass.

"Rien—" her voice rose in panic.

"Don't worry, my little psycho," I said, stepping over to her. She swayed and fell, but I was there to catch her in my arms. "Don't worry."

Sara

Rien caught me as my legs buckled. He swept me up into his arms. I remembered him carrying me before. No. He couldn't have.

"I feel strange," I said, my tongue thick and mumbling.

"I've given you something," Rien said. He was carrying me back, back to the bedroom. The lights were dim but I could still see his face. It was impassive, relaxed.

"No—"

"It's a special dose. I hope it wasn't too sweet."

The cupcake. Oh, god.

"You drugged me," I moaned. I tried to twist in his arm, tried to get away. Was he really planning to kill me, just as Gary had said? Why had I trusted him? I hit his chest with my fist, but all my strength was gone. "You drugged me!"

"Fame is a drug. So is money. So is power. My drugs are just more effective, that's all."

He set me down on the bed and adjusted my dress. He towered above me and admired me, and fear and loathing mixed inside me with desire. Hazy and uncertain, I reached out and he took my hand. My fingertips buzzed with feeling, but I couldn't control my muscles.

"Let me put on some music," he said.

He left my side for a moment. Above, a classical guitar began to play softly.

"What is this?" I murmured. "What… what drug…?"

"Ecstasy, mixed with my own special blend of barbiturates and a bit of fast-acting muscle relaxant. It was in the raspberry coulis."

"Why?"

"Why the coulis? I thought you didn't like needles. I was doing you a favor."

"No. *Why?*"

I looked at him, trying to focus my eyes on his face. His golden eyes. Predator eyes. Eyes that wanted me. Eyes I wanted to stare into forever.

"Why did I drug you? So you'll tell the truth," Rien said simply.

I breathed in. Every breath was an ordeal.

"You don't trust me." I don't know if it was the drugs or not, but this was what made me feel the most disappointed. I'd thought that all of this—the blindfold, the shower, the dinner—was leading up to him trusting me. But no. It had all been a show, a ruse to lure me in. The song playing from the stereo was filled with a longing sorrow. I blinked slowly.

"I don't trust anyone. Nothing personal, my dear."

He raised my arms above my head. I pulled against his grip, but he was strong and my muscles were all jelly.

"Rien—"

"Don't take it as an insult, Sara. I only want to know what you know. And I think I know how to get you to tell me."

He was tying my wrists. I could feel rope being drawn across my skin. My head lolled up awkwardly and I saw him finishing the knot on my wrists.

"Try to get out," he said. I pulled my wrists apart, but they wouldn't move.

"No. No. Rien. Please."

He moved down to the bottom of the bed. His hand closed around my ankle, and I kicked, or tried to. I might as well have been kicking something underwater. Every part of me felt like it was moving in a dream. He pulled another rope around my ankle and tied it. My entire focus shifted to the pressure of the rope against my skin. He tied the rope to the bedpost and pulled it taut. Then the other foot. When he tightened the rope, my legs pulled apart and I heard the dress tear. I cried out. I was completely held down, vulnerable.

"I won't hurt you, my beautiful little psycho. You're too perfect. But if I find out you've been lying to me, well, then I might have to kill you."

I whimpered. What did he want from me? I'd lied, sure. I'd lied about being Susan. But if he needed to know where she was, then he was wasting his time. The ceiling spun above my head. I couldn't make my muscles obey me.

"Now, we're going to start with Susan. Tell me what you know."

"Nothing! I told you everything!"

He reached up to the bedside stand, going out of my vision for a moment. Then he was back. I saw what was in his hand and screamed.

"*NO! RIEN, NO! PLEASE!*" The scalpel flashed silver in the dim bedroom light. My scream was cut short as his other hand clamped over my mouth. My shrieks burned my lips but I couldn't break through his hand. A blinding white fear shook me.

"Oh, Sara," he murmured. "No, no, no, Sara. You have entirely the wrong idea."

My moan came out muffled against his hand.

"I said that I wouldn't hurt you. The drugs will only

last an hour."

He looked at me and I could not look back. I sobbed, twisting against the ropes.

"Oh, Sara, Sara. You don't trust me. How can I trust you if you don't trust me?"

He leaned forward, raising the scalpel up. I closed my eyes. Even with my eyes clamped shut, I felt like the world was spinning. Would it hurt? Would I feel it at all?

I felt the coldness of the blade running up my leg and his hand loosened over my mouth. God, was he cutting me along my side? I felt faint. Then a pause. I couldn't take it.

"Please make it quick," I whispered. "Just make it quick."

His hand was on my cheek. I opened my eyes to see his face hovering above mine, sympathy in his eyes.

"Sara, believe me. I only want the truth."

I heard the snip of the scalpel cutting through fabric, and he pulled off my dress. Green and gold, fluttering down to the floor.

"I want you to tell me the truth."

Another snip. My panties were gone. I whimpered as his hand moved up with the scalpel, but he was only putting it back in the bedstand.

"Can you do that for me? Tell me the truth?"

"I don't know what you want me to tell you."

He bent down and kissed me on the mouth. I turned my face away. He grabbed my chin with his hand and ran his thumb across my lips.

"You've done a very good job of pretending to enjoy my attention tonight," he said.

I wasn't pretending. My mind thought the words, but my lips couldn't form them in the air.

Then his hands ran down over my body and I shuddered all over.

"First, I think I'll make sure you're in the proper state for interrogation."

He pulled his tie off, and then laid it over my eyes. I jerked my head back, but he knotted the tie quickly.

I moaned. This blindfold wasn't like the cotton. There was no light coming through, and I couldn't see a damn thing.

"Don't," I begged.

"The drug will amplify your senses," he murmured. His voice was in my ear, echoing through my skull. "But I need you to focus."

His mouth moved down, biting my neck softly, nipping my skin. I moaned again and again as every touch of his sent another thrill spiraling through my body. His tongue licked me, then his teeth closed down on my arm. His hands were everywhere, stroking, squeezing. I was dizzy with it.

"Rien—"

"Where is Susan Steadhill?"

"I don't know."

"Wrong answer."

He licked my nipple, the light pressure making me harden instantly.

His hands fluttered over my skin. Everything he did was gentle, barely touching me. Whatever he'd given me to drug me made everything seem a hundred times as intense. And this light pressure built my nerves up to a high-pitched tension. It drove me insane.

Then his tongue was at my entrance. He ran his tongue in light circles over my swollen nub. More, more, then—

He was gone. Nothing. No hands, no tongue. Nothing of his touched me. I cried, a keening cry that made my whole body shiver.

"Rien—"

"Where is she?"

I shook my head wildly from side to side.

"I don't know," I gasped. "Touch me, please. Please, let me come—"

"Not yet."

I could feel him loosening the ropes at my ankles. I pulled at them with my legs, and the knots gave way. I clamped my thighs together and squeezed. I could make myself come, I could, I knew I could. The drugs coursing through my system revved my adrenaline to full power. The ache heightened as I pushed myself closer... closer...

His hands grasped my hips, and he flipped my body over before I could finish. The rope tying my wrists together twisted against my skin. I whimpered, and he spanked me hard.

"*AH!*"

His fingers teased me at my entrance, only slipping in slightly before withdrawing. I cried out, moaning. He spanked me again. The pain shot down my leg, my skin burning with the impact.

"Susan. Where is she?"

"No, no." My mind was gone, spinning out of control. I couldn't focus on anything but the touch of Rien's fingers. He spanked me harder, over and over again. Each time he did, his fingers slipped in a bit farther into me, and I'd think that he was going to let me come. Then he would withdraw, and slap me, and the bright pain made me ache even worse.

I wasn't me anymore. I was a hollow shell that only he could fill. I needed him. My body ached for him. I wanted him to bring me to the edge and past it, to leap off into the abyss with him inside of me.

"Susan."

"I was Susan. I was supposed to be Susan." My characters! They were all falling away from me. I had nowhere to hide.

"Where is she now?"

"Don't... Don't know." I thought hard. Where was she?

The touch of his hands sent my focus spiraling off into the spot where my thighs met my ass.

"I don't know where she is, oh God, Rien, please, I don't know where she is."

"Will you tell other people about me?"

"What?"

"If I let you go."

Let me go? He was thinking about letting me go? I gasped. I couldn't keep my thoughts straight, but this one reverberated through my system.

"You're going to let me go?"

"Would you want that?"

"Yes."

"Would you go to the police if I let you go?"

"I... I don't know." I thought about Mr. Steadhill. He was an asshole, sure, but I couldn't leave him tied up to be tortured and killed. But no, it was Rien asking me. Rien. I had to tell him no. He wouldn't let me go if I didn't. But I couldn't make myself say the words.

One word, Sara: NO.

I couldn't do it. I couldn't lie to him.

"Would you tell them about me?"

"Will you let Mr. Steadhill go?" I asked. Maybe if he did that, then I could say that I wouldn't go to the police.

"No."

"Oh, I can't. I can't. Rien—"

"You would tell them about me? The police?"

"Yes. No. Yes, I would." The words caught in my throat. I couldn't lie. Whatever he had given me had muddled my brain and the lies were gone, no matter how I grasped for them.

"I'm sorry, Rien," I gasped. "I'm sorry. I would

have to."

"Thank you, Sara." His mouth was at my ear. "I believe you."

"Are you going to kill me?" My mind spun.

"No. Not if I can find Susan."

"Please, Rien—"

"Do you want me to stop now?"

"*No*." I was panting. I needed him.

His chest was hot on top of my back. This time though, his cock was sliding against my ass, and—*oh! God!* The tip eased forward into me, pressing for entrance.

"I believe you, Sara. This is only for you now."

My mouth went dry.

He pushed into me with one sharp thrust. I gasped as I felt myself expand, clenching around him. He paused there, and I shuddered. Every twitch of my muscles sent different signals through my body. After a few seconds, he moved again.

"*Ohhhh*," I groaned.

Inch by inch, rocking back and forth, he worked his swollen cock deep into my ass.

I screamed. I begged.

Every second felt like an hour. He spanked me, pinched me, kneaded me. The world disappeared as he edged inward; everything around me was a void and we were alone in it. My nipples ached with the mounting pressure. Then he thrust forward again and I clutched the sheets and screamed.

His hand reached around to my front. When his fingers brushed against my stomach, it tickled; I yelped and yanked against the ropes, but they held.

"Rien!"

He slipped his hand down and cupped me, and my shout turned into a moan. Dark, it was so dark.

His two fingers slicked both sides of me even as he

worked his cock in deeper. I bucked my hips, hoping for him to touch me, but he pinned me down and spanked me hard.

"Be good," he whispered.

"Good…" I moaned. I wanted more, I *needed* more. Still, I was shocked when he reached down and curled two fingers, thrusting them into me. I jerked back.

Slowly, firmly, he rocked his hand back and forth. The melody slowed, matched his rhythm, and it seemed like he was conducting both of us, me and the musician.

I lost myself completely in his grip. Rocking, moaning, I moved along with him, his hips rolling against mine and stretching me impossibly, then withdrawing so slowly that the terrible agony of the friction sent my body into shudders. Again, again, he thrust inward, and as I breathed in I could swear that the oxygen had all gone from the air. In the dark, unable to see, I imagined myself sucking in an airless vacuum of space.

Then my body came screaming back to me as the pressure built, built, the ache turning me into a gibbering, needful monster. Rien's fingers thrust faster and faster, beating in a different time along with his pumping cock. I gasped and gripped the sheets on the bed between my fingers. My wrists strained at the ropes and my body stretched to its limits and then just beyond, the pain shimmering right above the pleasure.

Now. I whispered the word in my mind, and then it needed to be true.

Now. Now. *Now*. The ache was too much. I needed him. I needed Rien to take me, to throw me off of the top of this shaking cliff.

"Now," I strained. Rien thrust deep and bent his mouth to my ear.

"Now?"

"Yes, yes, oh God, yes. Now, yes. *Now!*"

Blind and bound, I writhed endlessly. My body was wracked with my terrible, dark need: the need for *him*. His cock urged on deeper inside me, his fingers teased me to the edges of sanity. I screamed and his hand wrapped around my throat, my scream turned into a cry of ecstasy, filling the room as I exploded in pure pleasure. So bright it was soundless, and even the music in the room seemed to stop for that second, that endless, endlessly delicious second where reality disappeared and everything was wonderful and Rien was wonderful, the whole world a wonder.

My screams subsided, the shivers ran through my body. My nerves tensed and hiccuped. Rien's arms closed around me and held me close. His palms felt burning, beautifully hot. I gasped for breath as he caressed me and squeezed me softly against him. His cock was still hard, pulsing, but he held me and did not push in.

My heart slowed, and the music came back into focus. The beat of the drum, so much slower now than a few minutes ago. The drugs must be hitting my system, now, I thought slowly. Then I laughed at myself.

"What do you want?"

I blinked dreamily. Rien's voice came into focus as though it was visible in the air. Like floating letters spelling out his question.

"Nothing."

It was my automatic answer. I didn't want anything. I never did. I don't owe anyone any favors. I did right by my family by not wanting anything.

"What do you want? Sara?"

My consciousness slipped back and forth between two worlds. In one of them, Rien was touching me, his voice gentle in my ear. His lips fluttering kisses down my chin. The sheets were silken, like lying on doves' wings. The music playing lilted in the air, a guitar stringing a note along for eons, singing just for me.

In the other, my hands were knotted above my head, and my legs were stretched apart with ties. Rien was stretching my body, torturing my senses, his thick cock penetrating me. The rope was rough against my skin. The beat of my pulse thudded in my ears.

The two worlds refocused into one.

"Yes."

"Tell me what you want."

"I want you. Only you. I love you. Oh, Rien. *Rien—*"

He groaned. His hot seed burst into a strange part of me. I shuddered with him as he pumped into me one last time, my body gripping his cock hard before it slipped out. Every cell in my body seemed to quiver with complete satisfaction as he held me, this killer, this lover, held me and did not let me go.

CHAPTER TWENTY-THREE

Rien

It would be easier if she lied.

I admit, I half hoped that I could kill her. But she was perfectly honest. More than that, she wanted… me.

Her body unraveled under me, and I could only lie there and hold her as she shivered into my chest. I had taken her apart, my toy, and found the truth I'd been looking for.

Now I had to face it.

I had taken an innocent girl hostage. Hell, I'd almost killed her without knowing. I felt sick just thinking about it.

My hands untied the ropes binding her to my bed automatically, without thought. I took off her blindfold. She stretched, all feline curves and sensuality, and rubbed the raw part of her wrists where she had pulled against the bindings.

I was emotionally drained and physically exhausted. Her body would rid itself of the drugs soon, but I felt as though I needed stimulants to carry me through what was to come. I had to find Susan Steadhill if I could ever let her leave. I would go tonight. I'd stop by Jake's and ask him personally if he had any leads. He hated calling over the phone; he insisted that the government monitored every word.

I had to find her. I had to kill her and kill Mr. Steadhill. Then Vale would get off of my case and I would be able to think clearly about all this. I wouldn't have to kill Sara if I could find Susan. I couldn't let her go, but at least I wouldn't have to kill her.

She yawned, her hand brushing my back, and I lay down beside her, cradling her. So innocent. The way she looked up at me, I could swear that she actually loved me. After all that; after I'd teased her and tortured her for the truth. Guilt flooded my system.

"I have to tell you something, Sara," I said.

"Yes?"

"I have to keep you here. With me."

She blinked drowsily.

"I am here with you."

"I know. And I want to let you leave. Eventually. But now, I can't. I have to find Susan Steadhill." I got up, pulled my clothes back on.

"Now?"

"Yes." I buttoned my shirt up. She watched me, her tongue wetting her lower lip as I buttoned the top button. Maybe there was another way. Maybe I didn't have to let her go.

"Sara, you said you loved me."

She blushed. Oh, hell. My cock stiffened again at the bashful look on her face.

"Do you... would you want to stay here with me?"

"What do you mean?"

The look in her eyes: fear. She was scared of me. And rightfully so. I couldn't ask her to stay in a prison indefinitely.

"Never mind."

"Rien—"

"Never mind. We'll figure it out later."

"Do you want me to sleep here?" she asked, frowning.

"Do whatever you want."

She sat up, pulling the sheet around her body. Bending down, she stooped to pick up the green dress.

"I think… I think I'll sleep in the library." Her eyes didn't meet mine. Jesus. If she had told one lie, it had been that. Maybe she had loved the sex; whatever it was, her feelings had obviously vanished along with the drugs in her system.

"Do you need me to help you there?" I asked.

"I'm fine."

"The door will lock behind you automatically."

"Okay," she said softly. She stood up to leave. I didn't watch her go.

In the bathroom, I splashed water on my face. I rubbed my eyes and stared into the mirror. Who was the person staring back? Some idiot in love. Some fool who thought he could keep a real girl in a fake prison. How had I fallen for her so bad? I sighed. One mistake, and all my life's work was in jeopardy. One stupid, beautiful mistake.

Sara

I went back into the library, the sheet draped around my shoulders. My head was spinning. I had told Rien I loved him. He wouldn't let me out, though. Wouldn't let me out unless—

He had to know where Susan Steadhill was. Okay. I had an idea. It wasn't a great idea, but it was a start.

I pulled on the green dress. Rien had slit through the strap, so I tied it back together. There. I wasn't presentable, but at least I wasn't buck naked. The silk fabric fluttered against my ankles.

I opened the bookcase and tiptoed through. Outside of the window, the lights of Los Angeles twinkled in the night.

Mr. Steadhill was sleeping on the operating room

table. I took a deep breath and pulled off his gag. He yelped, and I shoved the gag back in, putting my finger to my lips. He stared at me with one good eye, then nodded. I eased the gag back up.

"Listen," I whispered. "I think I've figured out how to get out of here."

"You have?"

"There's another way, through the front," I said, making every detail up as I went along. If he believed me, he might tell me how to reach his wife.

"Untie me and we'll go."

"I can't. He—uh, he's got your vitals hooked up to one of the alarms. If you take them out, it'll go off."

"Who cares? I want to get out of here!"

"Anyway, the door to the library is locked."

"Library?"

"Shut up and let me talk!" I hissed, trying to make it seem like it was urgent. "I can't get back in. He's the only one with the key."

Mr. Steadhill frowned, and the scab above his eye twitched. My dress strap fell down and I pushed it back up.

"So what? You can't leave either? Why'd you even bother—"

"Wait. He lets me sleep in his bedroom. I can sneak out at night. I can't get you out right away, but I can get the police to come and get you."

"Alright."

"First," I said, hoping to God that he would play along, "I need to know where your wife is."

He fixed his eye on me, and the half of his face that still remained twisted into a scowl.

"I killed her."

Rien

Stupid me. Stupid girl.

I followed her to the library after a minute, just to make sure she hadn't tried to escape; it was silly of me to have let her out of my sight in the house. Even with the remaining barbiturates swirling in her system, she might have managed to lie.

Behind the wall, I could hear her moving around, and the door was locked tight. I considered opening up the door to talk to her again, but I didn't know what I'd say to her. There wasn't anything else to say, was there?

No. I had to go find Susan Steadhill.

I picked up my medical bag from the bedroom and made sure that I had all of the necessary supplies. A sedative preloaded into a syringe. I put it in my pocket for easy access. I checked once more that all of my security system was up and running. It wouldn't do to have her trying to escape. Everything checked out. Great.

Heading out, I flipped off the lights and opened the front door. I dropped my bag to the ground in surprise.

Vale was standing in front of me. He raised his gun to my face.

"Where exactly do you think you're going?"

Sara

I stared down incredulously at Mr. Steadhill. My mind reeled.

"You... you killed her?" I felt like retching. I felt

like he'd stabbed me in the gut. It was him. Mr. Steadhill. He was the murderer.

I felt completely betrayed. Rien would have let me go, but I felt terrible about letting Mr. Steadhill die without doing anything to save him. Now, though... he'd killed her. I couldn't think anymore.

"She was sleeping around behind my back. When I confronted her, she said that we would split after we got to Brazil. She would go her way, and I'd go mine."

I swallowed, trying not to seem too shocked. My brain raced a hundred miles a minute. I had to hide my true feelings from him, or he wouldn't talk to me. Killer. Killer. That was all I could think. He killed and lied and lied about killing. He was the murderer.

"You didn't want her to come with you to Brazil, then?"

"Are you kidding? That stupid whore. She deserved to die."

I swallowed back my disgust. He'd killed Susan. He might have killed me before fleeing to Brazil. Would he have killed me? I was the only one who would have known about him. Looking at his leering eye, I would have sworn that he could read my mind.

I shut out those thoughts from my mind. There was only one thing I needed to know.

"Where's the body?"

"What?"

"Your wife's body. Where is it?"

"Why do you want to know?" His one eye squinted suspiciously at me.

"Look, this place is on lockdown. Even if I go tell the police what's going on, they'll come by and ask Rien and he'll just lie to them. It'll give him plenty of time to kill you and get away before they get a search warrant."

"You don't think they'll believe you?"

"The police? I could just be another L.A. loon

making up stories to get attention. But if I can show them a body, they'll come in here guns blazing. It'll give you a better chance, at least."

"But then…" Mr. Steadhill coughed. "They'll know I killed Susan."

"I'll tell them that it was the doctor who did it. Once they have hard proof, they can bust through the door and save you. Come on! It's our only chance!"

It was a story that I hoped he would believe. After a short pause, he nodded. Relief flooded my system.

"Okay," Mr. Steadhill said. "Okay. I—"

The door to the library burst open. I grabbed the nearest scalpel off of the medical table, ready to defend myself. Ready for anything. Or so I thought.

CHAPTER TWENTY-FOUR

Rien

"Vale, you gotta stop showing up like this." I stared past him. There was nobody else around.

"You have the teeth?"

"I'll get them for you. Tomorrow."

"Now."

"You said tomorrow."

"That's what I said before. Now I'm saying tonight. Where are you going, Rien?"

"Can't a guy go out for the night?"

"With a bag full of medical supplies and a syringe in his pocket?" His eyes darted down to my shirt. "Take it out."

I pulled the syringe from my pocket and put it down slowly on the floor.

"Vale—"

"I don't want any more lies. Get back inside."

I turned around and went back into the house. He closed the door behind him.

"I got some bad vibes off of you last time we chatted," Vale said, his eyes sweeping the house. "So I thought I'd come over a bit sooner and make sure you weren't going anywhere. Lucky me, huh?"

"I'll get you the teeth, Vale. By tomorrow."

"See, I want them now."

"I can't."

"Why not?"

I sighed. I couldn't lie to him forever.

"There's a girl."

"A girl?" Vale cocked the gun.

"Not Mrs. Steadhill. The wrong person came."

"The surveillance tapes showed—"

"She was an actress. Pretending to be Mrs. Steadhill."

"Alright." Vale looked like he was trying to sort the whole mess out in his head. "Okay. So the rumors were true after all. Susan is somewhere out in the world, maybe dead, maybe not. Where is she?"

"That's who I was going to go looking for," I said. I hoped he would let me go. Give me some time to figure out how to deal with it. Even if the best way was to run away from Los Angeles entirely.

"Where's the girl?"

"She doesn't know anything. She's innocent."

"You didn't kill her yet?"

I leveled a gaze at him.

"I'm not that much of a sick fuck, Vale."

"Right. You're such a bleeding heart. You know what this means?"

"I know what it means."

"Must be some girl, that you can't kill her. Show me."

"She's locked up in the library, okay? She doesn't know anything."

"Show me."

Sara

I gasped as Rien burst into the room. There was another man holding a gun to his head.

"Well, great. Now she's seen you too," Rien said to the man. "Are you happy now?"

"This is the girl?"

"Rien?" I asked, the scalpel shaking in my hand.

"It's alright," Rien said. He turned to the man who still held the gun trained to his head. "This is the girl I was telling you about. Sara."

"Doesn't look like she doesn't know anything," the man called Vale said. "Looks like she knows a lot, actually. Looks like she's standing over a dead body."

Mr. Steadhill moaned and the man stared in awe at the operating table.

"Are you serious?" he asked. "That guy is still *alive*?"

I couldn't stop staring at the gun that was pointed directly at Rien's head. I wanted to scream, to rush over and save him. He looked so calm, like he wasn't worried at all about the muzzle of the gun against his skull. But I was terrified for him.

"Help me," Mr. Steadhill rasped.

"They're both alive?" Vale turned to Rien, shoving the gun harder against his temple. Rien's head tilted to the side and my brain went blank. "Are you fucking kidding me? I'm going to kill you, I swear to Christ I will. *Both* of them—"

"Mrs. Steadhill is dead," I said quickly. My heart was thudding in my ears. He couldn't kill Rien. *No.*

"Don't tell them! Why would you tell him?" Mr. Steadhill said, his scream echoing in the operating room. I could feel the panic rising in my throat. "You bitch! You stupid—"

I shoved the gag in his mouth with my free hand. My hand holding the scalpel was still shaking, but I couldn't put it down. I was scared to death that Vale would pull the trigger. I was scared I wouldn't be able to defend myself.

"He killed her," I said. "Not Rien. Mr. Steadhill. He killed his wife."

"Oh, that's just lovely," Vale said. "Good thing I came here to get all the answers to my questions. I knew there was something going on with you, Rien."

"Please," I said, stepping forward. "Don't shoot him."

"What are you, the fucking police? No. I'm the fucking police." Vale pulled a second gun from his jacket and leveled it at me. "And look at this. Now I'm going to have to kill both of you stupid fuckers."

"Vale—"

Was that a flash of fear in Rien's eyes? Panic choked me.

"Shut up, Rien," Vale said, hitting him on the back of the head with the barrel of his gun. The crack of the barrel against his skull echoed across the room. Rien winced in pain and I shrieked.

"Don't! Don't kill him!"

"Shut up, both of you!" Vale screamed.

"Why?" I gasped.

"Why?"

"Why—why do you have to do this?" My throat was closing up, but I couldn't just stand here and die.

"Let me put it simply, sweetheart," Vale said. His voice was lower, but somehow that seemed even worse. "This—" he waved one gun in the direction of the table, "—is a goddamn mess. Here we have a special ops who can't do his fucking job of killing people, even though that's the thing he loves best."

He smacked Rien again on the back of the head with the gun and blood ran down Rien's cheek. I wanted to attack Vale. I had just met him, but I wanted to punch him through the face. He leaned forward and yelled into Rien's ear.

"I'm not even supposed to know about it, but I do. Because I'm the one who sends you jobs. Only you haven't done your goddamn job!"

"Vale—" he started, but Vale cocked the gun that was aimed at me and Rien's mouth slammed shut. He looked more terrified that Vale would shoot me than anything else.

"I'm sorry, Rien. You've been good. It's been good working with you. But this is a mess I need to get rid of. I've got a federal witness half-dissected on an operating room table who just admitted to killing his wife, whose body I'm *still* missing."

I inhaled sharply. He had been about to tell me. He had. I racked my brain for what I could do to make Vale stop.

"And we've got a civilian who's going to blab about this whole fucking thing to Rolling Stone so she can get her name in the papers."

"I won't!" I cried.

"Yeah? You're an actress. You're smack dab in the middle of a murder scene. You'd get a shitload of attention if you spread this shit around. And what, you're just going to frolic out of here and not tell anyone? I don't want to kill you, darling, but there's not a lot of options here. I'm sorry, I really am. If there was any other way, I would take it."

"Trust me, I won't—"

"How do I know I can trust you? Huh? Convince me."

"I—"

"Five seconds to convince me. Or I start my cleanup with the good doctor here."

How could he trust me? I couldn't let him kill Rien. I couldn't let him kill me. I saw Rien breathing deeply, and I could see the terror in his eyes. I looked down at Mr. Steadhill, who was still straining against the straps. And I knew what I had to do.

Stepping forward, I pressed the scalpel against Mr. Steadhill's neck. And I followed the line Rien had drawn for me.

CHAPTER TWENTY-FIVE

Rien

I gaped as blood spurted from Mr. Steadhill's neck.

"What the _fuck_," Vale gasped beside me. He lowered his gun to his side, amazement on his face.

Sara stepped back, the front of her green dress already soaked in blood. The scalpel dropped to the floor with a clatter.

"Sara—"

I rushed to her side. She stumbled back, clutching at my arms, and I caught her. Blood pooled on the ground, and Mr. Steadhill's eye stared up blankly at nothing. He was dead. Sara bent over, retching air. I held her by the waist. Finally she shuddered and stood up shakily. She looked at Vale.

"I won't. Tell. Anyone."

"Jesus," Vale said breathlessly. "Jesus."

Sara swallowed, her eyes darting back to the blood that still dripped from the table.

"There," I said to Vale. "Are you satisfied?"

"What about Susan Steadhill?"

"I think… I think her body is under the Santa Monica pier," Sara said. She spoke softly, but in the silent room her voice carried.

"Did he tell you that?"

"No, but when we first met, he said that that's where they went before their last fight. I didn't think anything of it, but… but…" Her teeth chattered, and her whole body shivered again. She couldn't stop staring down at the dead body.

"It's okay," I said, pulling her close to me. "It's okay. It's all over now." I looked up at Vale. "Right?"

Vale licked his lip, staring first at the body, then up at me. "Sure. Yeah. Right."

I turned Sara away from the operating room table. I led her into the waiting room, out of sight of Mr. Steadhill. She sank wordlessly into a chair.

"Stay here," I said. "I'll be right back."

Her pale face stared up at me. All of her strength seemed to have left her. Her arms hung loosely at her side.

"You're going to be okay," I said. "I'll just be a minute."

I left her sitting there and went back to the operating room. Vale had taken a pair of pliers and was yanking a molar from the mouth of Mr. Steadhill. He put the bloody tooth in a ziploc and tucked it away in his back pocket.

"Thanks for the proof," he said. "Next time make it a little cleaner, okay?"

"Yeah. Are we done here?" I asked.

"Sure," he said. I walked him out of the operating room and to the door.

"I can't believe she killed him," Vale said. He shivered. "Just a swipe of the blade, and—"

"I can believe it," I said. "You goaded her. A civvy. She thought she was going to die."

"Yeah, well, like you said, it's all over now."

"I won't tell if you won't," I said. "Would you really have killed her, though?"

"An innocent girl? You know me, Rien. I'm a sucker for pretty faces."

"Sure," I said. I didn't know if I believed him. Good as I was at telling faces, Vale was a pro at concealing his thoughts.

"I would have killed you for sure, though," he said. "Don't lie to me again."

"Don't send me the wrong person and I won't lie to you."

"Okay. Yeah. I'll let you know once we have the other body," Vale said.

"I don't care. Just let me know once you have another client for me. If we're still working together."

"We're still working together. Rien?"

"Yes?"

Vale shook his head, putting his gun away in his jacket.

"You have fucked up taste in women."

"Trust me," I said. "I'm as surprised as you are."

Sara

I sat in shock in the waiting room. There was a body in the room next door. I'd killed him. I'd killed Mr. Steadhill. Bile rose in my throat and I turned my face away from the door.

"Sara?"

I jumped in fright, but it was only Rien at the doorway.

"Will you give me a second?" he asked. "I'm going to clean up, okay?"

I nodded mutely. He closed the door. I could hear him moving things around. Was that the sound of him wheeling the body somewhere? I wondered how he would get rid of it.

All of my system was in shock. I couldn't feel anything. There was a buzzing in my ears. I stared at my feet. The broken shards from the glass globe were swept up in a neat pile in the middle of the floor along with the little plastic pieces. He hadn't thrown any of it away yet.

Minutes passed. Then the door opened again. Rien's hands were clean but there was blood on his shirt, a dark stain near his heart.

"It's okay now," he said.

"There's blood on your shirt." I pointed to his chest.

He immediately unbuttoned his shirt and turned to go back into the other room. I heard the sink running. When he came back, he was wearing a new shirt, crisp and clean.

"Better?" he asked.

I nodded. He walked over to me and put his arm around my shoulders as though I was a fragile piece of glass. Despite myself, I leaned into his embrace.

"Do you want me to take you home?" he asked.

"I… I don't know."

"Do you want to leave?"

I opened my mouth, but no answer came out.

"You don't have to leave, Sara," Rien said.

"It's just… there's nobody I can talk to about this," I said, my voice catching in my throat. My skin burned. I had nobody to talk to outside of here. My mother didn't know anything about me. Neither did my sister. I'd kept my life a secret from them. I'd kept my true self hidden away for so long that there was nobody left to share it with.

"You can stay for as long as you want."

Stay? Stay? What was I thinking? But every part of my being longed to stay here, with him. In this moment, he was a comfort. A known danger. And, heaven forgive me, he looked at me like he wanted me to stay.

"I feel like I'm going insane," I said. "Am I going insane?"

"No, you're not. The first time… it's hard."

I began to cry, hiccuping back my sobs. Rien held out a handkerchief and kept his arm tight around me as I sobbed into the white cotton square.

"It's alright," he said. His hand rubbed my back, and oh! I wanted to melt into his warm strong palm. I wanted to melt away completely. The image of blood filled my mind and I struggled to fight it. There was so much blood. I clutched the handkerchief to my face as I cried and cried and leaned into him.

"I did it," I moaned.

"It's alright."

"I did it. I killed him."

"He had to die. One way or another, he would have died."

"But…"

"I'm not going to tell you not to feel bad about it. You'll feel however you want to. You're the one who killed him."

Killed him. Killed him. Killed him.

"Sara, listen to me."

I snapped back to attention. Rien's eyes settled on mine, searching.

"What are you looking for?" I asked.

"I'm not sure."

"I'm a murderer now. Do I look different?"

He shook his head sadly.

"You did what you had to do, Sara."

"I couldn't— I couldn't—" I choked on my sobs. My body collapsed against his and he held me so tightly that it didn't matter that I was falling.

"What is it?" he whispered. His arms felt warm around my shoulders, his chest broad and sturdy. I leaned against him and let my tears fall. My fingers twined blindly around his, and he kissed the tops of my knuckles. My cheeks were hot and wet and I could barely get the words out.

"I couldn't… watch you die."

Rien

She stayed to talk. I put another log on the fire, and we sat on the rug together in front of the flames. She cried. I held her. As the flames burned down, her eyelids fluttered, drooping.

"I can't fall asleep," she said.

"Is it because you're not in bed? "

"No. I feel like if I fall asleep, something terrible is going to happen. I'll wake up and everything will start all over again from the beginning." She looked down at her right hand, the one she'd killed Mr. Steadhill with. Her fingers flexed.

"I won't let anything happen to you."

"I know," she said. "I still worry. Would you…"

"Yes?"

"Would you inject me with a sleeping sedative?"

I raised my eyebrows.

"I thought you were afraid of needles."

"I was. I'm not anymore."

"No?"

"Maybe I am, but sometimes you have to do what has to be done."

"Is that right?" I asked, squeezing her on the arm.

"Yeah," she whispered. "That's right. I just want it to go away, Rien. Just for a while."

"Then let me carry you to bed, and I'll inject you with whatever horse tranquilizer it takes to chase the bad dreams away."

"Alright," she said. She yawned when I picked her up, her eyelids drooping shut. Her head knocked against my chest as I walked, her hand clutching my bicep. And by the time I rested her head against the pillow, she was already sound asleep.

Sara

The next day, I woke up in an empty bed. Rien was gone. I wandered around the house, but he wasn't anywhere. I went to the front door and tried the knob.

Unlocked.

The door swung open, and I squinted into the brightness of the Los Angeles sunshine. I could hear the roar of the freeway in the distance.

I closed the door.

Rien found me sitting in the waiting room, putting his sculpture back together. I'd gotten rid of the glass shards, and I was trying to rebuild the artwork piece by piece. Without the globe to hold it together, it was hard to figure out how it could work.

"Here," he said, handing me a tube of superglue. "Let me help."

We worked side by side in silence. The little pieces built up one by one, and with the glue we were able to remake the globe without the glass around it. Rien put the last piece on top, holding it until the glue dried.

"It's not quite perfect," I said, rocking back on my heels to look at the sculpture. The broken pieces made it look like the top of the artwork was flying off in all different directions.

"No?"

"It doesn't look trapped anymore."

"That's fine," Rien said, squeezing my hand. "That's better than perfect, my love."

"Don't call me that."

"My love? What else should I call you?"

I shook my head wordlessly.

"What else but my love, my dearest, my beautiful?"

Tears welled in my eyes. He didn't mean it. He couldn't.

"Rien, don't—"

"You are my everything. My indescribable pain and my everlasting pleasure. My passion and my fear. My angel. My joy. My little psycho."

"Rien…"

"You are mine, all mine, every last bit of you, no matter when you decide to leave."

I turned to him, tears welling in my eyes. He bent and kissed me, his lips asking softly for permission.

"My love," Rien said. "Do you want to leave?"

"No," I said truthfully.

"Then stay," he said, and kissed me again.

EPILOGUE

Sara

It's been three weeks, and I haven't gone home. I still have dreams at night, bad ones. When I kick and scream, Rien puts his arms around me until they stop. Sometimes he cries out in his sleep, and I'm the one who comforts him.

He asked me if I wanted to leave the day after I killed Gary Steadhill. He's asked me every morning since then. And every morning I say no.

Why?

Out there, out in Hollywood, I was a fake person. I had fake friends and fake ambitions. Here, though, all of that drops away. I'm only real when I'm with him.

His lips draw real pleasure from my body. His fingers caress my curves and I know without a doubt that he wants me and that I want him. His mouth makes mine scream.

He holds me down, his hand on my throat. He ties me up whenever he wants to, and teases me until I beg him to take me. He makes me scream until my throat is hoarse and my body aching for release, and then he throws me off the edge of the abyss and comes along with me.

If I ever want to leave, I know that he will let me. But right now, I'm still deciding what I want. Really, truly want. And it might be that what I want isn't a Hollywood ending. It's not perfection, because nothing perfect is real, and I can't be fake anymore.

It's not a prince and his princess, and it's not a happy ever after. It's two people with nothing to lose and everything to gain, holding onto each other for dear life, their bodies trembling together in the darkness.

And maybe that's all I ever wanted.

The End

Thank you for reading MINE

If you enjoyed the story would you please consider leaving a review on your favorite retailer?

Just a few words and some stars really does help!

Also, be sure to sign up for my mailing list to find out about new releases, deals and giveaways!
http://bit.ly/ADarkNewsletter

Made in the USA
Lexington, KY
14 October 2017